A mere week ago, chiding herself to

To take risks and reap the rewards. Now here she was, practically in the arms of the most alluring man she'd ever known. All it would take was a step forward.... She stretched up to press her lips to his, although she might have lost her nerve if he hadn't leaned down to meet her.

After one stunned second of paralysis, she closed her eyes and gave herself up to the moment, the once-in-a-lifetime chance to live out cherished fantasies. Wrapping her hand around his neck, she stood on tiptoe and kissed him, dizzy with sensation.

Carpe Dylan.

Dear Reader,

Have you ever wanted to be someone else, just for a day? That's the premise I started with for *Mistletoe Cinderella* and the character of Chloe Malcolm. She's brilliant, gifted with computers and has a wry sense of humor (once you get to know her). But back in high school she wasn't the kind of girl who could catch the eye of baseball star Dylan Echols.

Ten years later, at her high school reunion, Chloe shows up with a makeover courtesy of her fairy godmoth— Er, best friend. Dylan notices her, all right, but confuses her with somebody else entirely. When midnight strikes, will she turn back into plain old Chloe?

My mom, who has a great sense of humor, raised me on funny, romantic films of mistaken identity like Doris Day's *Lover Come Back* and the more recent *While You Were Sleeping*. I hope you enjoy *Mistletoe Cinderella* as much as I've always enjoyed those charming, feel-good movies! And I hope you'll watch for the summer installment of my 4 SEASONS IN MISTLETOE miniseries, *Mistletoe Mommy.*

Happy reading!

Tanya Michaels

Mistletoe Cinderella

TANYA MICHAELS

TORONTO • NEW YORK • LONDON
AMSTERDAM • PARIS • SYDNEY • HAMBURG
STOCKHOLM • ATHENS • TOKYO • MILAN • MADRID
PRAGUE • WARSAW • BUDAPEST • AUCKLAND

Recycling programs
for this product may
not exist in your area.

ISBN-13: 978-0-373-75259-1
ISBN-10:   0-373-75259-8

MISTLETOE CINDERELLA

Copyright © 2009 by Tanya Michna.

www.eHarlequin.com

Printed in U.S.A.

ABOUT THE AUTHOR

Tanya Michaels started telling stories almost as soon as she could talk...and started stealing her mom's Harlequin romances less than a decade later. In 2003 Tanya was thrilled to have her first book, a romantic comedy, published by Harlequin Books. Since then, Tanya has written nearly twenty books and is a two-time recipient of the Booksellers' Best Award as well as a finalist for the Holt Medallion, National Readers' Choice Award and Romance Writers of America's prestigious RITA® Award. Tanya lives in Georgia with her husband, two preschoolers and an unpredictable cat, but you can visit Tanya online at www.tanyamichaels.com.

Books by Tanya Michaels

HARLEQUIN AMERICAN ROMANCE

1170—TROUBLE IN TENNESSEE
1203—AN UNLIKELY MOMMY
1225—A DAD FOR HER TWINS
1235—MISTLETOE BABY*

HARLEQUIN TEMPTATION

968—HERS FOR THE WEEKEND
986—SHEER DECADENCE
1008—GOING ALL THE WAY

HARLEQUIN NEXT

DATING THE MRS. SMITHS
THE GOOD KIND OF CRAZY
MOTHERHOOD WITHOUT PAROLE

*4 Seasons in Mistletoe

Don't miss any of our special offers. Write to us at the following address for information on our newest releases.

Harlequin Reader Service
U.S.: 3010 Walden Ave., P.O. Box 1325, Buffalo, NY 14269
Canadian: P.O. Box 609, Fort Erie, Ont. L2A 5X3

This book is dedicated to all of you
wonderful readers who e-mailed to ask,
"Will there be more Mistletoe stories?" Enjoy!

Chapter One

It was a bad sign when you were feeling envious of the person in the casket.

Chloe Malcolm winced at her own thoughts, which were highly inappropriate and completely out of character. Chloe was *always* appropriate; it was one of the things Aunt Jane had teased her about. Swallowing a knot of emotion, Chloe smiled at her aunt's peaceful face. As far as Chloe knew, Jane Walters had never once in her sixty-three years worried about decorum. It was that free-spiritedness Chloe envied.

Aunt Jane had appalled Chloe's parents by nicknaming her niece "Wheezy," making the childhood asthma Chloe later outgrew seem like more of an in-joke than a handicap. *I'm going to miss you.* Jane hadn't spent much time here in Mistletoe—too busy running with the bulls in Pamplona or, more recently, hot-air ballooning over Flagstaff—but each of her visits had been memorable.

"How are you holding up?"

Chloe turned to see blond and beautiful Natalie Young, her best friend and manager of the town's flower shop. "Okay. I know she wouldn't have any regrets and wouldn't want any of us moping. She was just so full of *life* that it's hard to believe…"

"Yeah. She was a force all her own." Natalie grinned. "I'm amazed at some of the stories I've heard this afternoon, but I guess you grew up with them."

Not exactly. Chloe's parents had loved Jane, but they hadn't minded her keeping a geographical distance from their impressionable daughter and had deemed some of Jane's exploits unfit for young ears.

Back in the sixties, Aunt Jane had shocked her own parents and her older sister when she'd eloped with a local boy who'd left shortly after for Vietnam. When he'd come back, he'd been unable to assimilate to small-town Georgia life; he and Jane had restlessly roamed the country for the remainder of their marriage, part of which she'd spent dancing in a Vegas show and perfecting her blackjack skills. Chloe's mother, Rose, had commented more than once that her younger sister had the devil's own luck. She'd said it with neither jealousy nor censure, but worry. Fear that Jane's exuberant, outrageous ways would catch up to her one day.

But Chloe believed Jane left this world exactly as she would have wanted—after a day of parasailing in the Caribbean and a romantic evening with a forty-nine-year-old divorced tax attorney, she'd died of a blood clot in her sleep. Jane had dated a wide range of men in the past two decades, never lacking companionship. She'd aged beautifully, like Helen Mirren or Diane Keaton. Still, Chloe thought that what really attracted admirers was her aunt's confidence and verve—two qualities Chloe lacked, except when it came to computers.

During Chloe's teen years, Jane had insisted her niece was simply a "late bloomer." At twenty-seven, Chloe had resigned herself to the fact that she was as bloomed as she was going to get.

Trying to push away vague pangs that she might have let her aunt down, Chloe redirected her attention to Natalie. "The arrangements are beautiful, by the way. I'm sorry I didn't say so earlier."

"Thanks." The blonde pursed her lips. "You don't think the flowers seem too formal? I filled people's orders, but I feel like Jane would have preferred sunflowers or daisies. Something bright or funky. The remembrance wreath and spray of rosès are a little at odds with…everything else."

"Like the music and the open bar? I thought Mama would have a conniption."

Jane's final wishes had been well-documented with her lawyer, right down to the slide show and five-song sound track for the memorial. It had been designed to follow Jane's life, ending a few minutes ago with "Spirit in the Sky." But it was the earlier "It's Raining Men" that seemed to have left an impression on guests. Jane Walters hadn't wanted a funeral; she'd wanted a party at which the people she'd known could celebrate her life. If she'd picked out Chloe's attire for the service, it probably would have been the flowered sarong Jane had once sent her niece from Maui. Instead, Chloe had paired a lightweight blouse with her navy skirt, her only touches of whimsy the polka-dotted yellow headband holding back her long dark hair and pomegranate-flavored lip gloss.

"Speaking of your mother." Natalie looked around. "Is she doing all right?"

"Hard to say." Chloe's parents, aside from making sure their only child knew how adored she was, didn't make a point of discussing their emotions. What Chloe had deduced for herself was that restrained and proper Rose, dutiful first daughter, had always had a complicated relationship with her free-spirited younger sister. "Mama mentioned that she didn't think Jane had ever truly stopped loving her husband and that the two of them can be together now. She was talking to some old schoolmates the last time I saw her, but I should check on her."

As soon as Chloe said *school,* Natalie opened her mouth.

Chloe headed her off at the pass. "Let's not discuss the reunion now, okay?"

"Of course not." Natalie's blue gaze was suddenly bright with innocence. She should have joined drama club as a student instead of the cheer squad. "I wouldn't nag you at your aunt's memorial service."

A refreshing change. Natalie had been nagging on a daily basis since she'd signed on as a committee member for the Mistletoe High reunion. During their senior year, Natalie had made a few uncomfortable attempts at socially assisting Chloe, her erstwhile algebra tutor, but had felt ever since graduation that she, as popular cocaptain of the cheerleaders, should have done more to boost her nerdy friend's status. Whenever Natalie talked about the reunion, she got an overzealous gleam in her eye and morphed into a stubborn fairy godmother hell-bent on dragging Cinderella to the ball. Nat harbored unrealistic dreams of making Chloe over so that everyone could be dazzled by her a decade later, the once-shy brunette voted prom queen or reunion queen or whatever.

"Girls." Vonda Kerrigan approached, nodding her respects. In her midseventies, Vonda was closer to Rose in age but closer to Jane in personality. The two women had shared a cheerful disregard for conventionalism and had spent time together whenever Jane visited town. "Kasey and Ben are taking me home now, but I wanted to say goodbye to you, Chloe."

Chloe hugged the older woman gently. "I'm glad you came."

"Wouldn't have missed it." Vonda's wizened face split into a grin as she looked over her shoulder at the bar and handsome bartender. "Even from the hereafter, Jane throws a good party. You know, I think she accomplished just about everything she wanted to during her lifetime. Not many people can say that."

True. Some people had difficulty even figuring out *what* they wanted, much less achieving it.

Vonda patted Chloe's shoulder. "I can see a little bit of her in you."

Chloe smiled politely. She wanted to be flattered by the comparison, but it was too hard to believe. *I couldn't be less like Aunt Jane if I tried.* Chloe's idea of rebelling was taking two complimentary mints instead of one after her Greek salad at the deli. When it came to dealing with programming errors or challenging code,

Chloe was self-assured and quick-thinking. When it came to tackling life…

Well, she could learn a thing or two about living from the dearly departed.

THREE DAYS LATER, as she returned from running errands, Chloe discovered that Aunt Jane didn't just throw parties from the hereafter—she sent gifts.

Chloe had worked at home that morning, updating pet-sitter Brenna Pierce's professional Web site and brainstorming ways to incorporate new features Brenna wanted to add. Then Chloe had joined her parents for lunch at the seniors' center. Mr. and Mrs. Malcolm had moved into a small apartment in the complex last winter, deeding Chloe the modest two-bedroom home she'd grown up in and explaining that it was getting difficult for them to maintain the house and yard.

"We're not spring chickens, you know," her dad had joked.

Because Chloe had been an unexpected late-in-life baby, her parents had always been much older than those of her peers. When she was little, she hadn't noticed, but the first time she ever spent the night at Natalie's, she'd been struck by the difference. Natalie's mother had double-pierced ears and laughed as she asked them who the cutest boys were at Mistletoe High.

Dylan Echols.

The name rose so suddenly in Chloe's mind that she almost tripped over a crack in the sidewalk. Other female classmates might have sighed over the Waide brothers or brooding and vaguely dangerous loner Gabe

Sloan; in Chloe's mind, however, there'd been no contest. Dylan Echols was the best-looking guy in all of Mistletoe. But her unrequited infatuation had been ten years ago—he'd left town after graduation on an athletic scholarship. Though she'd seen him since then in the newspaper and on television clips, he rarely visited Mistletoe. Surely she'd moved on from an unrequited adolescent crush?

Then again, it was difficult to move forward when you spent your time with the same people year after year, had barely updated your wardrobe to reflect the new millennium and lived in exactly the same place. She frowned at the house, and a brown box on the porch caught her eye. *Was I expecting a delivery?* Not that she could remember. Curious, she quickly took the three steps leading up to the front door. The label was penned in familiar loopy cursive. Although Chloe's middle name was Ann, the packages always came addressed to Chloe W. Malcolm.

W for Wheezy, an epithet that was suddenly, alarmingly appropriate.

Chloe's chest had tightened at the sight of her aunt's handwriting, and for a moment she couldn't breathe. She sat on the top step and closed her eyes, waiting for the initial panic to pass. The more she fought for air, the worse the situation became. Besides, this was not one of the long-ago respiratory incidents that had landed her in the E.R. or prevented her from chasing other kids in the neighborhood while they played tag. She was just temporarily dazed.

Intellectually she knew that packages from other

countries could get held up in customs and take extra time to reach their destinations. *Emotionally* she was startled to be receiving mail from someone she'd said her final farewells to over the weekend.

After a moment, Chloe stood, fishing her keys out of her windbreaker pocket. She carried the box inside, set it on the kitchen table and stared at it. Then she picked up the cordless phone and dialed.

"Mistletoe Berries and Blooms," Natalie chirped on the other end.

"Hey, it's me." Chloe sagged into one of the straight-backed chairs that had been in the kitchen since the late eighties.

"Chloe! I was going to call you later. You won't *believe* what came in the mail."

"She sent you something, too?" Unusual but not unheard-of. Jane had been generous as well as spontaneous. "Because I have to tell you, I'm a little—"

"She who? I was talking about a him."

"Oh. I got a package today. From Aunt Jane."

"Wow."

"Yeah."

"What did she send?"

"I haven't opened it," Chloe admitted. "Knowing it's the last one of these I'm going to get, it felt disrespectful to tear into it like a five-year-old at a birthday party. But treating it with a lot of pomp and circumstance seems silly when, for all I know, it's an obscene T-shirt she thought was funny." Chloe had two such ribald tops from New Orleans that she'd never wear in public. Heck, she practically blushed just sleeping in either of them.

"I'll close the store early and come over."

"You sure?" Chloe asked, grateful but feeling melodramatic.

"Yeah. It's been kind of slow today. We did some nice spring arrangements just before Easter, but it won't get seriously busy again until prom, Mother's Day and summer weddings. I'll be so swamped in June you'll forget what I look like. Give me about half an hour, okay?"

True to her word, Natalie showed up right at the thirty-minute mark. She was holding a bag from the local grocery.

"Provisions," she declared. "They're not perfect, but it was short notice."

Once inside the kitchen, Natalie pulled out a plastic container of macadamia-nut cookies and piña colada wine coolers. Chloe smiled at the impromptu tropical theme.

Natalie opened a wine cooler and passed Chloe the still-cold bottle, then opened one for herself and held it aloft. "To Aunt Jane."

"To Aunt Jane."

They clinked the bottles together and each drank. Then Chloe slit the packing tape with one of the kitchen knives and pulled back the cardboard flaps. On top was a postcard, showing a beautiful white sandy beach and crystal-blue waters. Chloe flipped it over.

I got you a card with a half-naked cabana boy, but then kept it for myself. Put this by your computer and daydream about future vacations. I saw the enclosed dress and thought of you—you still don't know how beautiful you are. Give some

*local fellow a chance to show you! Or come with
me to the tropics, and I'll introduce you to a nice
cabana boy. I'm proud of you, Wheezy, but don't
spend all your time at the computer and taking
care of your parents! Shake things up from time to
time.*

   Love and mai tais,
   Aunt J

Chloe had to blink away tears to read the end of it,
but she grinned when she got there. She held the
postcard out to Natalie.

A second later, Natalie chuckled. "Think there are
cabana boys in heaven?"

"If not, Aunt Jane's talking Saint Peter into it even
as we speak."

"So what's this dress look like?"

Good question. Chloe pushed aside some plain tissue
paper and got a glimpse of deep red. The silky material
slipped through her fingers like water.

"Whoa," Natalie said, looking over her shoulder.
"Now *that's* a dress."

Chloe held it up, stunned. Her aunt had seen this and
thought of *her?* Perhaps Jane had been under the influence
of a mai tai at the time. The so-called sleeves were wide,
off-the-shoulder bands, hardly more than straps; the skirt,
while the same color, was a different material. It fell in
gauzy, staggered layers to form a handkerchief hem. Even
at its longest point, the skirt would barely reach her knees.

"Try it on," Natalie urged. "That's what she would
have wanted."

"I'm not convinced it's my size," Chloe said. The hours she did on the treadmill to improve her lung capacity kept her trim, but the skirt looked brazenly insubstantial. And the draped neckline—which wouldn't come anywhere near as high as her neck—didn't seem big enough to hold in generous C cups.

Natalie rolled her eyes. "It's not like I asked you to show up for dinner at the Dixieland Diner wearing it. It's just us."

"All right, all right." Chloe took the dress back to her room without further protest. She shrugged out of her clothes and eyed the red fabric. *Here goes nothing.*

Not only did the dress fit, it looked as though it had been magically tailored to her body. Surprised, she turned in front of the mirror, enjoying the way the fabric moved. When Vonda had said she could see some of Aunt Jane in her, Chloe had dismissed it as a well-meaning fib. Now though…

"This is not a Chloe dress," she told her reflection. It was beguiling, just for this moment, to see herself as someone else, someone—

"I'm going out of my mind with curiosity," Natalie complained from the other room.

"Come take a look," Chloe called, doing mental inventory of her closet. What kind of shoes did one wear with an outfit like this? She doubted canvas sneakers would cut it.

From the doorway, Natalie reiterated her earlier assessment. *"Whoa."* Then she grinned. "We have so found your outfit for the reunion."

"Natalie—"

"Explain to me why you won't go," the blonde demanded, her hands on her hips.

Because high school had represented some of the most abysmal times in Chloe's sheltered life. In elementary school, she'd been mostly invisible, the girl who sat quietly in class and read storybooks through recess; she'd never minded. The only child of a couple who hadn't expected to be blessed with a baby, as well as being born premature and battling respiratory developmental delays as a kid, Chloe had received *tons* of attention at home. Not being the center of everyone's focus at school had been a relief.

Her teachers liked her well enough and she made good grades. Maybe she hadn't been invited to a lot of roller-skating and swimming parties, but she wasn't that coordinated anyway. She'd buried herself in descriptions of faraway places and made lots of fictional friends.

Then came her teenage years. As a freshman, she'd had a significant growth spurt, and was suddenly several inches taller and filling out her blouses *much* differently. Also, there were far more extracurricular activities offered in high school. Teachers were no longer content to inconspicuously give her A's—they asked her to peer tutor and courted her publicly for events like the Academic Decathlon. Although her parents' official policy was that Chloe couldn't date until she was sixteen, they'd allowed her to go to the fall homecoming dance sophomore year and meet a boy from her geometry class there.

That dance had been a fiasco. Chloe had been

nervous, awkward within her changing body and with the sudden attention of classmates who'd previously ignored her. Her date had grazed her breast at the punch table—which she realized in hindsight had been an accident—but she'd jerked away violently enough to send Candy Beemis, a popular brunette, sideways into three dozen filled and waiting cups. Candy went on to cocaptain the varsity cheerleading squad, so one would think she could forgive a less socially adept person an awkward moment.

One would be wrong.

Instead, Candy and her A-list entourage targeted Chloe for snide comments. What Chloe had hated most wasn't that they cracked jokes at her expense, but her own inability to quip back or at least to shrug it off. She froze every time, her throat tightening as her cheeks heated. Natalie, annoyed with Candy's pettiness and exasperated by Chloe's tendency to react like a deer in the headlights, had claimed that Candy was jealous. Chloe couldn't imagine what kind of insane person would have been jealous of *her* in high school.

And now Nat wants me to willingly relive all those superfun glory days?

Chloe sighed. "Our former classmates fall into two groups. Those who had no clue who I was and those who ragged me about who I was."

"A-*hem*."

"Not counting you," Chloe amended. "You are a true friend."

Although it *had* been Natalie's idea senior year to give Chloe highlights, neither girl knowing that Chloe's dark brown hair had natural red undertones. The proposed blond touches intended to make Chloe glamorous had become clownish orange streaks that sent Candy and others into fits of giggles. Fairy godmothers were supposed to transform pumpkins for you, not give you pumpkin-colored hair.

"You're a successful self-employed woman who can seriously work that slinky red number you're wearing," Natalie said. "Don't you want to stick it to everyone who heckled you by showing up and looking hot?"

She hated to think she was insecure enough to need that kind of validation. "Stick it to them? It's been ten years. I don't care that much about anyone's opinion. Especially at seventy-five dollars a ticket."

"Well, that includes a sit-down dinner and dessert buffet. Don't forget the great band. And it goes without saying that the floral arrangements will be phenomenal." Natalie smiled beseechingly. "Come on! There have to be some people from our graduating class you want to see."

"Most of the people I care about still live here in Mistletoe."

Natalie's blue eyes took on a wicked gleam, but she ducked her gaze, making a point of studying her French manicure.

"What?" Chloe demanded. "What ace do you think you have up your sleeve?"

"I got an unexpected RSVP today. From Dylan Echols."

Dylan? An all-too-clear picture of his sexy grin and deep green eyes flashed through Chloe's mind. "He's really coming home?"

After college, the former Mistletoe High baseball star had become a local celebrity when he worked his way through the "farm system," pitching two and a half seasons in the minors before being called up to play for the Atlanta Braves. As far as Chloe knew, he'd been back in Mistletoe only once, for his father's funeral this past January. That had to have been a dark period for him, coming on the heels of a highly publicized early retirement. He'd torn a rotator cuff last season. After surgery, time off and physical therapy, he'd attempted to return but it was clear his pitching arm would never be the same. Just when Dylan had, according to sports journalists, "hit his stride," his dreams of becoming the next Nolan Ryan or Greg Maddux were snatched away.

"I'll bet Dylan would *love* that dress," Natalie added. "You could really wow him. A little red lipstick, we could do something special with your hair…"

"I prefer my usual gloss," Chloe said. Natalie had given her a gift certificate two birthdays ago for a fancy cosmetics Web site, and she'd developed a fondness for their line of high-end flavored glosses. "Remember what happened the last time you got big ideas about my hair?"

Natalie had the grace to blush. "Well, maybe someone at the salon could help you with it this time."

"Yes, but why? What's the point of spending three hours trying to convince a guy who doesn't remember me that I'm someone I'm not?"

While Chloe had adored Dylan from the back of civics class, he'd given no sign of reciprocating the sentiment, which would have first required him to notice her existence. He'd been preoccupied with either baseball or whichever girl he'd been dating that week. Dylan Echols was the kind of guy who'd held court in high school, a student-body Prince Charming who made peers and teachers alike laugh during discussion and led his baseball team to state championship.

"Are you sure *you* know who you are?" Natalie asked skeptically. "Jane saw that there was a lot more to you than just a quiet straight-A student. I do, too."

Chloe remembered the way she'd felt at the memorial service, the vague sense of having let down Jane. *I could be more, couldn't I?* Suddenly she found it difficult to recall why she was so set against going to the reunion. After all, it was just one night. Seventy-five dollars wouldn't break the bank.

Still, she worried about Natalie's plans for the evening getting too grandiose. "I'll go. But stop imagining some movie where the formerly mousy heroine shows up, impresses everyone with her poise and scintillating conversation and wins her man. Get real. Dylan's only going to be here for the weekend, and he doesn't even know me."

Natalie smiled, undeterred. "Then we'll have to find the perfect opportunity for you to introduce yourself."

Chapter Two

Dylan Echols muttered a word under his breath that network censors would definitely frown on. Since the broadcast had just gone to commercial, however, he felt free to express his irritation.

And Grady Medlock, seated behind the anchor desk, was free to snicker. "The scores may not be as important as world politics," Grady said, "but viewers still expect you to get them right."

Dylan didn't bother responding. The newscaster had been insufferable ever since Dylan was hired, and had become even more so since Liza Finnell—the object of Grady's unrequited affections—had hinted at the station's spring picnic last month that she was attracted to the newest addition to the Channel Six team. Dylan had ducked her interest by politely reminding her that he was seeing someone.

At the time, anyway.

As of Friday's e-mail, his brief relationship with Heidi was over. Dylan wasn't sure what bothered him the most: that she'd jilted him for a Braves first baseman he himself had introduced her to, that she'd jilted him via an impersonal e-mail or that he'd only recognized in hindsight that she'd used him as a stepping stone to better-paid guys who were still in The Show.

Dumb. Much like the mistake he'd just made in his broadcast.

For the majority of Dylan's reports, he had plenty of time to prepare beforehand, but he'd flubbed some incoming college scores on the teleprompter. Falling back on adolescent habits, he'd made a joke to cover his unease reading aloud. Why had he thought this local sportscaster position was a good idea? *Because you didn't have a Plan B.*

He'd known what he wanted to do with his life ever since he pitched his first elementary school baseball game, striking out older kids with more practice. He'd known the major leagues were his destiny, but he'd had no idea what to do when the glorious ride screeched to an abrupt halt.

Liza, the divorced hair and makeup artist with a bright smile and a kid, darted forward to give Dylan a powder touch-up. He wondered if he would ever adjust to having to use on-air cosmetics. *Pretty boy,* his father would have sneered. *More looks than brains. Thank God you have a decent throwing arm.*

"Great job tonight," Liza offered.

"Really?" He was careful to keep his tone teasing, not want to take his annoyance out on her. "What broadcast have you been watching?"

"Your recovery was fantastic. Don't let Grady bother you. He's a jerk."

Dylan flashed a quick smile. "That's nicer than what I usually call him."

Grady Medlock was an insecure windbag who clung to the hope that covering important events made *him* important by extension. He'd been none too thrilled when Channel Six hired an ex-Braves player whose minor celebrity status threatened his own. Dylan sympathized with having insecurities, but he had no patience for men who puffed up their own egos by belittling their team-mates.

The commercial break ended, and the cameras cut to the weather segment. Dylan could seethe in peace until it was time for the entire Channel Six crew to bid viewers good-night. As he stood, unfastening his lava-lier mike, he noticed Liza hovering to his left at the edge of the lights.

He chuckled at her anxious expression. "I'm not that upset. Don't worry about me."

"Is that how I look?" She smiled self-consciously. "You're probably sensing nervousness."

"About?"

"Asking you to dinner this weekend," she said in a rush. "My ex has our son for a couple of days, and you're not on the schedule, so… I heard about you and Heidi."

Who hadn't? His spotlight-seeking former girlfriend had thrown her arms around her new beau right in the middle of a postgame interview. Dylan winced. They hadn't been together long enough for him to be broken-hearted, but he hated to be humiliated. Though Liza's interest in him might be a soothing balm to the ego, this job was already awkward without adding the complication of dating a co-worker.

"Thanks for the invite," he said, "but I'm out of town this weekend. Going home." The word felt clunky and foreign on his tongue. Despite the years that had passed, his mother still called Mistletoe his home, as in *when will you be…?*

"Town in north Georgia, right?" Liza snapped her fingers. "Christmas? Evergreen?"

"Mistletoe." For such a small place, it held a vast store of conflicting memories. He'd struggled through his early school years—far worse than the actual dyslexia had been his father's disdain that Dylan couldn't read properly—but he'd later developed his fastball and his confidence. Most important, he'd been blessed with Coach Todd Burton's mentorship. The gruff affection of the high school coach, who was officially retiring this spring and would be honored at a dinner this weekend, had almost made up for Dylan's uncomfortable home life.

Almost.

Liza nodded. "Well, have a good time."

"Thanks." High school *had* been a good time. He'd set the division record for strikeouts but never struck out with his female classmates. He'd graduated with an indulgent fondness for Mistletoe High, grateful for what had taken place during the four years but knowing he was headed for bigger things.

Now he was returning, a twenty-seven-year-old has-been. Would he enjoy the reunion? He didn't want to be one of those clichés who stood around all night with a beer in hand, reminiscing over former glory. For a second, he regretted his RSVP.

However, on the heels of his breakup, it seemed like a good time to get out of Atlanta for a few days, and his mom deserved better than to be neglected by her only child. In earlier years, he might have resented that she hadn't done more to intervene, buffering him from his emotional bully of a father, but it was hard to be angry when she seemed so lost without her late husband. Dylan planned to stay at the reunion hotel, visiting the house to see his mom and find out if there was anything she needed done around the old place. The moment of the weekend he most looked forward to and simultaneously dreaded was presenting the appreciation award at Coach Burton's dinner. Perhaps more than anyone else in the entire town, Coach had believed in him. Dylan was sorry that two shoulder surgeries hadn't been able to keep their combined dream a reality.

He grimaced at the weekend that stretched ahead. If he were *really* lucky, his mother would be in a cheerful, noncloying mood, the reunion band would be loud and the hotel would be filled with pretty alumnae feeling nostalgic.

"I CAN'T BELIEVE you talked me into wearing these!" Chloe stepped out of the car, hyperaware of the towering heels she'd borrowed. She'd accepted Natalie's red shoes and patient help with a curling iron, drawing the line at crimson lipstick and salon highlights.

Natalie grinned as she handed her keys to the valet. "I can't believe it, either, but you look great."

Chloe tottered into the lobby, trying to adjust to Natalie's expensive pride-and-joy shoes. Natalie had said she was glad *someone* could wear them tonight since they wouldn't have matched her sapphire-blue spaghetti-strapped dress. Ironically, the appreciative way the hotel clerk behind the counter followed Chloe with his eyes did nothing to bolster her. Women like her aunt knew how to gracefully handle attention; Chloe always felt breathless and panicky. Why couldn't she have been more of a "people person" like Jane or Natalie? Even Chloe's professional contact with clients was done largely through e-mails, rather than face-to-face.

"I tell you what," Natalie said sympathetically, "let's check to make sure there aren't any last-minute glitches with the reunion committee or hotel staff, then I'll buy you a drink in the lobby bar, okay?"

"Deal." Chloe followed her friend downstairs, fighting the urge to tug at the top of her dress. She'd never left the house with this much cleavage exposed.

One floor below the main lobby, an elegant corridor led to the ballroom. Waitstaff in white tuxedo jackets were setting tables in the back half of the room. Toward the front, a stage set with sound equipment overlooked a portable dance floor. An archway had been created with tightly fastened helium balloons of green and gold, their alma mater's colors. Against the entrance wall was a long table covered in a gold cloth and rows of name tags. A man and woman, both in formal attire, stood near it.

Natalie headed in their direction. The man was Jack Allen, who had been their student-body president and was now a married father employed by the planning office of city hall. The striking dark-haired woman next to him was—*ugh*—Candy Beemis.

Though Chloe had seen her former nemesis around from time to time, they hadn't spoken since high school. Candy was the personal assistant to one of the town's wealthiest women and spent most of her time in elite circles. Well, as elite as Mistletoe got, anyway. The brunette's shimmering white one-shouldered dress looked like a toga as reimagined for the Academy Awards. Annoyingly, she hadn't gained a visible pound in the past ten years.

"Hi." Chloe smiled in their combined direction but focused on Jack's congenial face.

He returned the smile, his gaze apologetic. "You'll have to forgive me, I'm blanking on who you are."

"Chloe. Chloe Malcolm?"

"Right. Sorry. I'm terrible with names. My wife harasses me about it constantly. I have entire building forms memorized, but can forget our neighbor's name in the middle of a barbecue." He turned to Natalie, reporting on the event's status. "Everything's well in hand. We had to make a quick appetizer substitution, but they're not charging us extra. Candy was just on the phone with the band's lead singer. ETA is about ten minutes for sound check."

"Nat, you did such a darling job on the flowers," Candy interjected with a toss of her sleek, shampoo-commercial hair. "One of these days I'm going to have to develop an actual skill. And, Chloe! I hear you're quite the entrepreneur. If I had it to do all over again, I'd go the computer-nerd route myself."

No, you wouldn't.

Even though Candy's tone was playful, no overt malice, Chloe bristled. It was one thing for Natalie to call from the shop, freaking out because the computer had crashed and she needed the help of a "professional geek." Yet being reminded of all the times Candy had indeed made Chloe feel like a socially awkward nerd—and encouraged others to treat her as such—was different.

Behind her polite smile, Chloe ground her teeth. She gestured toward a table covered with a green cloth and Mistletoe High memorabilia. "I think I'm just going to stroll down memory lane."

As the reunion committee finished their conversation, Chloe idly studied framed pictures from pep rallies and school plays. Gold and resplendent, the trophy from the state baseball championship sat in the center of the table; the Academic Decathlon first prize she'd helped win sat off to the side. Still, she grinned at the unlikely parallel of her and Dylan Echols, school superstars. *And here I thought we wouldn't have much in common to discuss.*

Beyond the mementos Natalie had convinced the high school to let them borrow sat rows of name tags. Leaning over for a closer look, Chloe realized that each tag was printed with a black-and-white yearbook photo and identity: *Chloe Ann Malcolm.* Period. She hadn't flown high enough on the social radar to earn the Most Popular, Most Likely to Succeed or Most Likely to Make You Laugh labels that accompanied some of the other names.

Natalie had not warned her that she'd be walking

around all night with that awful senior portrait pinned to her chest. *Eek.* In Chloe's junior picture, she'd removed her glasses and squinted, so she'd overcorrected the next year. With her wide eyes, lopsided formal drape and mouth caught between forced smiles she couldn't hold long, she looked surprised and frightened of the photographer. Not flattering.

The silver lining had been that shortly after Chloe's parents had seen the picture, they'd finally allowed the contact lenses she so desperately wanted.

Surveying the photos of her classmates, she stifled a laugh. She wouldn't be the only one regretting her senior photo. In his shot, Brady Callahan sneered at the camera, his hair teased into short spikes and his eyes rimmed with black eyeliner; he'd long since outgrown his Goth phase and was a deacon for a local church. A few students who'd been into grunge at the time proved that what looks trendy one day merely looks like an aversion to hygiene the next. Of course, Natalie, blond and smiling, looked perfect in her picture. All the cheerleaders did.

If it weren't for Nat being her best friend, Chloe would have suspected the squad of making some sort of demonic pact. It seemed statistically unlikely that not one of a dozen teenage girls had blinked, had a bad hair day or had a zit.

Chloe found herself studying the row of *E*'s, telling herself she wasn't looking for anyone in particular. But she knew that was a lie even before her gaze landed on Dylan's photo. Though the black-and-white photo didn't do justice to his green eyes, there was the promise of sexy intensity he'd later grow into, and that one left dimple made visible by his cocky grin. Seeing that smile in class had turned her knees to jelly. Their civics teacher had once called on Dylan, who'd clearly been flirting with a redheaded volleyball player instead of listening; when he'd floundered for a response, Chloe had blurted the answer, bringing the moment to a quick close. The teacher had frowned but returned to the lecture. Dylan had turned slightly, sending a smile in Chloe's direction and a bolt of lightning straight through her.

Emotions were often exaggerated for teenagers, though, distorted through a hormonal lens. She was an adult now, not an overreacting adolescent. If she happened to glimpse Dylan's smile in the crowd tonight, she doubted lightning would strike again.

"You ready for that drink?" Natalie asked from beside her.

Chloe jumped. "I didn't realize you were there."

"Too preoccupied with—" Natalie smirked at Dylan's name badge "—memory lane?"

"Watch it, smart aleck. I may decide to go home early—like now."

"I have the keys, remember?"

"So your whole 'let's do makeup at my house and ride over together' suggestion was a trap?" She'd been wrong—this wasn't Cinderella at the ball, it was a hostage situation. Technically Chloe could call a cab, but they both knew curiosity would keep her here until she saw him.

Chloe sighed. "What do you suppose it is about our

teenage years that we never quite shake?" Even her more recent memories from the nearby college she'd attended weren't as vivid as the day her team won the Decathlon or the day she'd realized Natalie, a teacher-assigned tutoring pupil, had become a true friend. Thinking about how much she valued Natalie, she smiled. "Tell you what, the drink's on me."

There was a private bar in the corner of the ballroom, but it wasn't staffed yet. They turned toward the doorway, Chloe's ankle momentarily twisting in the unfamiliar shoes. Wincing at the brief flare of pain, she regained her balance before she fell. *You can lead me to the Manolo box, but you can't make me walk gracefully in three-inch heels.* She made sure to hold the stair rail on the way up to the lobby.

The recessed lounge was an elongated rectangle a few steps down from the main entrance. Natalie gestured to a row of four high tables against the wall. "Grab us a spot, and I'll order."

"But I said I'd buy," Chloe reminded her.

"Well, I said it first. Besides…"

Chloe raised an eyebrow. "You don't want me pushing my luck balancing in these shoes, do you?"

"So, um, white wine? Or has the red dress inspired you to have something crazy and bold like shooters?"

"What do you think?"

"Two chardonnays coming right up."

Chloe pivoted toward a table at the far end, near an unmanned baby grand piano. She pulled herself up onto one of the two padded chrome stools at the tall table, taking the opportunity to slide off the red high heels.

Her feet were wider than Natalie's and the shoes pinched slightly. Also, Chloe was surprised she hadn't suffered a nosebleed from the extra height. She rotated her ankles and flexed her toes, closing her eyes in blissful relief. Now all she needed was a hot, sudsy bubble bath and the assurance that she wouldn't have to go anywhere near her senior yearbook photo ever again.

Her skin prickled, and Chloe opened her eyes, discomfited by the sudden sensation that she was being watched.

She saw him in the lobby, knew who it was immediately even though she couldn't quite believe he was really standing there in jeans and a green shirt. Dylan's gaze locked with hers, and electricity gathered, heavy and crackling. Sizzling energy ribboned through her.

Definitely lightning.

Chapter Three

Dylan had returned to the hotel depleted. Following an afternoon of physical labor—fixing a leaky pipe in his mom's kitchen, repairing the screen door—and emotionally taxing guilt that he didn't visit more, he'd walked into the lobby unmotivated to shower and change for the reunion. Suddenly, however, he felt pretty damn alert.

The shapely brunette in the bar area was a splash of vivid color among the black tables and chairs. She'd kicked off a pair of red shoes—he noticed them as his gaze traced over her long legs—and there was something invitingly uninhibited about her sitting barefoot in an evening dress. From what he could see, *everything* about her was inviting.

She had her head tilted back, eyes closed, a half smile playing about her full lips as if grinning at some secret only she knew. The neckline of her gown plunged just low enough to expose the shadow of cleavage and made his fingers itch to touch her. The thick mass of loose curls spilling past her shoulders looked as soft as her creamy skin. Then her eyes opened.

Although he couldn't tell their shade from where he stood, her startled expression as she caught sight of him was unmistakable. He was used to women doing double takes because they either admired him or recognized him. He was not accustomed to the alarm he saw on her features.

Because you were staring at her, Einstein.

The woman had opened her eyes to find a total stranger gaping at her from a few yards away. No wonder she was unnerved—although a lady who looked like that obviously got her fair share of appreciative glances. Now that she'd caught him ogling, he should go introduce himself as a nonpsycho, apologize with charm and offer to buy her a drink. This plan also meant he could look at her some more, up close. Bonus.

Then a blonde entered his line of vision, carrying two wineglasses. So much for buying the dark-haired beauty a drink. But he could still go say hi. The lighter-haired woman looked familiar, so maybe the ladies were from his graduating class, also here for the reunion. The women were holding whispered conference, and as he walked down the few steps that led into the bar, the blonde glanced over her shoulder. He definitely knew her.

Nancy? Nadia?

Natalie!

Natalie Young, he thought, recalling her name on the reunion literature he'd received in the mail. She'd been a cheerleader. He smiled, feeling a nostalgic warmth for the short-skirted green uniforms, each emblazoned with a sparkly gold *M*. The brunette had been a cheerleader, too, hadn't she? He'd been more interested in redheads back in the day, but he seemed to remember the other head cheerleader had been dark-haired and gorgeous.

Her name started with a *C,* didn't it? He struggled to recall it but was distracted. At this distance, he saw her eyes were an intoxicating whiskey color.

She leaned forward on the bar stool, toward him. "Dylan." His name rolled off her tongue in a husky voice weaker men called 1-900 numbers to hear.

For a moment he forgot Natalie stood there, almost between them. "Hi."

Natalie cleared her throat a little, sounding as if she were trying not to laugh. "Dylan Echols. Welcome back to Mistletoe. You might not remember me, but—"

"Sure I do." With effort, he took his eyes off the brunette. "Natalie Young. I remember both of you very well." They probably wouldn't appreciate his reminiscences over cheerleading outfits and the effect thereof on seventeen-year-old males.

"You *do?*" The brunette's sexy contralto had somehow become a squeak of disbelief—a damn shame.

"Absolutely." His smile was deliberately rueful. "A guy doesn't just forget two stunning women."

The dark-haired woman frowned at him over her wineglass. Did she think he was coming on too strong? Calling her stunning wasn't flattery, merely a statement of fact.

Natalie picked up her own wine. "Well, I hate to take my drink and run, but duty calls. I should get back downstairs and make sure my other committee members don't need anything. I'll see the two of you later!"

"But we just…" The brunette trailed off when it became clear her friend, already striding toward the stairs, wasn't listening. Then she—Connie? Caren?—turned back to him with a weak smile. Was it his imagination or had she paled? "You'll have to excuse Natalie. She lacks subtlety."

He grinned. "Not a problem. I've never been a big fan of subtle, anyway. To tell you the truth, I was going to take the straightforward approach myself, march down here and ask if I could buy you a drink, but—" Startled, he watched as she gulped down her wine in a manner he'd previously associated with keg parties.

She was either apprehensive or *really* thirsty.

Or perhaps she wanted the chance to take him up on his offer. Dylan signaled for a waiter. "May I join you?"

"Uh…sure. Suit yourself."

Well, there was an enthusiastic invitation if ever he'd heard one. Not quite a swing and a miss, but maybe a foul ball. *Hang in there, ace. You've come back from worse odds than this.* The waiter stopped at their table, and Dylan placed an order for a beer and a second glass of wine.

Once they were alone again, Dylan glanced down at the discarded heels beneath their table. "Nice shoes, but I—"

"I didn't want to fall down," she blurted before he could tell her that the barefoot look suited her.

Okay.

This wasn't going quite the way he'd envisioned. Maybe a smarter man would apologize for intruding, take his drink upstairs and get ready for the reunion, where there could be dozens of women interested in conversation. But it was suddenly, irrationally important to win over this one. Heidi's face flashed through his mind, followed by Grady's snickering. Dylan sought assurance that, in at least some way, he was still the guy he'd been before surgery, that he hadn't lost all his talents.

Besides, while he might tell himself that another man would walk away, he wasn't sure he had the will-power to do so. Not before he tried to cajole that husky tone from her again and bring a little heat to those skittish amber eyes.

THIS WAS LIKE a sick joke.

Which makes me the punch line, Chloe thought, drinking in Dylan's profile as he tipped the waiter. At first this had seemed exactly like one of Natalie's far-flung scenarios, a modern update of the fairy tales Chloe herself had loved to read as a girl: former geek, all dolled up, former athletic god walks into the room, their eyes meet…

And geek proceeds to trip over her tongue as if she's a fifteen-year-old on her first date.

She groaned at the unfortunately accurate analogy. All she needed to do now was crash into a refreshments table and this could be her first date all over again. What was wrong with her? Chances to live out long-held fantasies didn't come along every day. They barely came along once in a decade! But as much as she might admire Aunt Jane's brazen fearlessness or Natalie's ex-troverted ease, Chloe couldn't wipe away a personality years in the making and replace it as simply as if she were applying a new flavor of lip gloss.

"Everything okay?" Dylan asked. While she'd been lost in thought, he'd turned back to her, looking even more attractive than he'd been in high school. He was still lean and muscled, but his boyish charm had matured into an appeal that was adult and sensual. His black hair was as dark and thick as ever, and while she regretted his career circumstances, the disappointment seemed to have given him an alluring edginess, something he hadn't had as a seventeen-year-old golden boy.

And, wonder of wonders, *he'd* been attracted to *her!* She'd seen it in his smile when he first approached, before Natalie the Traitor had fled, abandoning Chloe to the butterflies in her stomach. It felt like she had enough in there for her own million-monarch migration.

"Ev-everything's fine," she said. Wow, repartee just didn't get any wittier than this.

There was no way Dylan had trouble getting women, so why was he still here, seeming…well, grimly determined to flirt with her? The situation had gone from being her wildest dream to her worst nightmare. Except that in her nightmare, she'd also be naked right now and late for a college final.

As awkward as things already were, why not just go ahead and lay her cards on the table? She took a deep breath—and a fortifying sip of wine. "Honestly? I'm a little nervous."

He grinned. "That's a relief. I was afraid maybe you didn't like me. Is it the pro-ball thing?"

"People here do consider you a celebrity," she said, noting how the brightness of his smile had dimmed when he mentioned baseball. "But no, that's not it. It's more the, ah, massive crush I had on you in high school."

Cards didn't get much more on the table than that. Aunt Jane would be proud.

"Really?" Dylan sat back. "If I'd known, I would have asked you out for a drink back then. The nonalcoholic type, of course. Maybe a milk shake," he added with a wink.

Gaping was probably not an attractive look for her, but she couldn't help herself. Did he seriously expect her to believe he would have dated her? "I didn't think I was…your type."

He looked sheepish. "It's true I dated a lot of redheads, but I noticed you, too. Every guy in the student body with working eyesight noticed you."

The warm glow she'd developed from thinking that Dylan might have returned her adolescent affections was cooling rapidly. Was he patronizing her?

"This may be coming ten years too late," he said, "but would you like to have dinner with me, Candy?"

She froze, confused. *Candy?* Oh God. Had he honestly mistaken her for Candy Beemis?

Under other circumstances, Chloe might have been flattered. Or at least amused. Right now she felt cruelly deflated. How had she let herself think, even temporarily, that he might really have remembered *her?* Now their stilted encounter was going to become more awkward than it already was. She would correct him, tell him she was Chloe Malcolm; he would frown and ask, "Who?" and she'd be crushed. It was one thing to know the boy of your dreams hadn't known you existed, it was another to have him verify it.

Stalling, she downed more of the dry wine.

Too bad it *wasn't* the ex-cheerleader sitting with him now. Candy probably knew how to handle a man's attention without dissolving into a flustered fool; she certainly would have had the chutzpah to wear the closetful of bold garments Aunt Jane had sent over the years.

"Is that a no on dinner?" Dylan asked, looking genuinely disappointed by her hesitation.

Dylan Echols wants to have dinner with me! Sort of.

Why, oh why, couldn't she have been someone else? Even if it was just for tonight. Someone comfortable enough in her own skin to wear red dresses and high heels and flirt with a sexy man. The someone Chloe had always longed to become but never quite managed. "No. I mean, it wasn't a no."

"Good." The grin he shot her was devastating; he should be required to carry a permit for using that on unsuspecting women. "I know we're both here for the reunion, but…I'm not in a crowd sort of mood. Were you looking forward to catching up with Natalie and the other girls from the squad?"

"Not as much as you might think."

"Would I be a jerk if I asked you to ditch the reunion and join me somewhere quiet where we can talk over a meal?"

"Sounds perfect!" For many reasons, including that it would only take him about two seconds downstairs to spot the actual Candy Beemis. Then he'd learn that

Chloe had been the nerdy girl in the back row who'd just admitted to being infatuated with him. *Pathetic*.

"So, do you still go by Candy or is it Candace now that we're all grown-up?" he asked.

She bit down on her lower lip so hard she half expected to taste blood instead of her chocolate-flavored gloss. "Actually…call me C.J."

Chapter Four

On the outside, Chloe was still smiling—she could feel it on her face, frozen like a mask. On the inside, she was screaming, *What did I just do?*

"What's the *J* stand for?" Dylan asked.

"Um…Jane?" Very smooth. With quick thinking like that, she'd missed her calling in some kind of under-cover career. Luckily he was finishing his drink, which spared her the follow-up question about why she was unsure of her own middle name. Hopefully he would attribute her uncertainty to the already confessed nervousness. *Get a grip. C.J. is not the nervous type.*

Whoever the hell C.J. was.

Out of the corner of her eye, she glimpsed a married couple she knew walking through the lobby—the man was another Mistletoe grad, and his wife had been toying with the idea of hiring Chloe to do a site advertising her homemade-cake business. Chloe ducked her head, letting her hair fall in a curtain across her face as she tried to monitor their progress surreptitiously. The longer she sat here with Dylan, the more she chanced one of their fellow alumni coming over to say hi. Of course, *anywhere* she went in Mistletoe…

"Dylan, do you have a room here at the hotel?"

He blinked at the breathless question, but his look of surprise faded into a slow grin. Oh Lord, had she just unintentionally propositioned the most eligible bachelor of her graduating class?

"Because I was thinking," she added in a rush, "about how you said you'd like to have dinner someplace quiet. Where we could talk. With you being a local celebrity, I thought our best chance at that might be room service. Unless I'm being too forward."

"No, I like a lady who speaks her mind," he assured her. "Room service is a great idea. That saves us the whole 'what are you in the mood for, what's good around here, no, you decide, I don't care' rigmarole."

Good point. If she was stumbling over questions like what her name was, she probably wasn't up for discussing where they should eat. She pushed her chair back, trying to seem cheerfully eager rather than desperate to flee. "I'm ready when you are."

He stood, but bent abruptly. "Don't forget your shoes." When he straightened, all the air around Chloe seemed to disappear. Natalie's red high heels had never looked as sexy as they did at this moment, dangling from their straps on one of Dylan's large hands.

Chloe tried to inhale, but her lungs must not have got the memo. When she reached out to take the designer shoes, Dylan's fingers brushed hers. A perfectly innocent touch. If Nat had called after a date, gushing about her hand meeting some man's, it would have sounded clichéd or exaggerated, but the lightning Chloe had experienced earlier just from looking at him now magnified and sizzled through every cell of her hyperalert body. *A body that's going to pass out soon if you don't* breathe, *you dummy.*

The unreality of the situation hit her, and she couldn't help smiling. "Thank you," she told him, her voice lower than she was used to hearing.

He grinned back. "You're very welcome. Here. Let me help."

There was no graceful and feminine way to get back into the shoes, and she gladly accepted his assistance, leaning on him as she stepped into the first, lifting her foot to wiggle the strap into place, then the other. Dylan Echols had his arm around her waist. *I can die happy.* The thought reminded her joltingly of Aunt Jane, but Chloe could easily imagine her aunt laughing at this entire turn of events. A wistful sense of envy edged through Chloe—her aunt had seized life even as a teenager, while Chloe had mostly survived hers by making safe, predictable choices. *Well, not tonight.*

She glanced from the elevators, which seemed like a portal to the deliciously unknown, to Dylan, who was just plain delicious. Smiling up at him with a flirtatious instinct she hadn't even realized she possessed, she asked, "Shall we?"

DYLAN HAD WITNESSED plenty of great comebacks in baseball—a team that was seemingly down for the count, turning it around in the eighth or ninth inning—but even he was amazed by the way his luck had turned tonight. Once C.J. worked past her initial timidity, everything had changed. She'd gone from looking terrified at the prospect of a meal with him to suggesting dinner alone in his room. Plus, she'd once again fallen into that sexy rasp he'd first noticed. Some guys were primarily visual creatures. Dylan himself had always been very tactile. He liked hands-on activities—his libido tried to suggest several—but he couldn't remember the last time he'd reacted so viscerally to just a woman's voice. It would be an actual pleasure to spend the rest of the evening listening to C.J. talk.

They headed for the elevators, falling into step, and she shook her head at him when he pressed the button for the fifth floor.

"You've probably stayed in some glamorous high-rises," she said. "Must be hard for the Mistletoe Inn to compete. Not a lot of penthouse suites here."

He chuckled wryly, thinking of some of the ratty places he'd slept when he'd played in the minors. "Trust me, I wasn't spending all my nights in five-star hotels. That kind of luxury is for guys who last more than a few seasons." And signed lucrative endorsement deals.

"Oh. Right." She bit her bottom lip, and he found himself staring. "Still, at least you've *been* places." She said it with admiration.

"Does that mean you stayed in Mistletoe?" he asked. Maybe that's what she'd meant about not needing to catch up with Natalie. Both women could still be local.

Before she could answer, the doors chimed and parted.

"This way." He gestured to the left and waited gallantly for her to precede him. Less gallantly, he noticed that she had a fantastic butt beneath the filmy red skirt.

That observation, combined with the act of unlocking his hotel room door, temporarily cast a different light on the moment. Normally if he was returning to a room with a lady… No, they were having dinner. He hadn't seen C.J. in ten years and unlike his newscasting colleague, there was a limit to Dylan's presumptuous ego.

Trying to think of something innocuous, he cleared his throat. "What do you do for a living?" His preference was always to discuss other people's careers, rather than his aborted one.

"I design—" From the way she broke off as they entered the room, he first assumed there was more to the statement. But after a beat, she simply reiterated, "I'm a designer."

"Fashion? Interiors?"

She laughed out loud, the musical sound making him smile even though he wasn't in on the joke. "Fashion, me?"

He lowered his gaze meaningfully over her dress. "Is it that hard to believe?" Then again, despite the stylish red garment she wore, it was indubitably the woman beneath the clothes who provided the va-va-voom.

His eyes met hers, which were bright with appreciation. Heat leaped between them, enough to prompt him to cross the room to the air-conditioning unit and lower the temperature. When he turned around, he noticed that she was studying her surroundings. He found himself relieved that he'd stopped by for only a few moments earlier, just enough to check in and drop off his suitcase.

Not that he was a slob, but boxer briefs over the back of a chair or dirty socks in the corner did not a romantic evening make.

"So." He rocked back on his heels. "Room service. The menu should be here somewhere."

The leather-bound menu turned out to be on a walnut-stained round table between two armchairs. He leaned against one seat, and C.J. took the other. He couldn't help glancing at her legs as she settled against the upholstery. Whatever exercise had replaced cheerleading in her adult life, her calves were smooth and well toned.

Thumbing through the menu, he asked, "Anything particular you're in the mood for tonight?"

He wouldn't have thought twice about the question except that she flushed a deep, rosy pink. His grip tightened on the room service folio as arousal filled him. She was so damned expressive, responsive.

She averted her gaze for a second, then grinned at him, appearing somehow both shy and mischievous. "Is this where I'm supposed to say, 'Oh, you decide'?"

"It's probably best if you don't," he said. "But I do have a few ideas."

Chloe was shocked by the blatantly suggestive teasing—mostly because she was actually participating. It appeared that "C.J." had a naughty streak. *Does that make me my own wicked stepsister?* Natalie was never going to believe any of this. Nobody in Mistletoe would.

"Should I order up a bottle of wine?" Dylan asked, scanning the list. "Or maybe a carafe?"

She gave a quick shake of her head. "No more for

me, thanks." As it was, she felt drunk on Dylan's proximity and ten years' worth of finely aged fantasies—not to mention two glasses of hastily quaffed chardonnay. What she needed now was to get some food in her system. She'd barely eaten today, distracted by primping and wanting to make sure the dress didn't bulge in the wrong places.

"Can I see that menu?" she asked, extending her hand.

"Absolutely." He passed it to her. "I think I know what I want."

Her heart thudded faster. Since when did everything sound like a double entendre? *Since someone as sexy as Dylan Echols is the one saying it.* The man could read aloud from programming manuals and make them sound hot.

After she'd decided on the steak salad and he chose the prime-rib dip, he called down to the kitchen.

He hung up the phone and smiled that same grin she remembered from civics class. "They said about twenty minutes. Can I get you something to drink in the meantime? I've got bottled water and colas."

"I could use a water, thanks." She closed her eyes for a moment. While the room wasn't quite spinning, it wasn't as stationary as she was used to, either.

Leaning into the minifridge, Dylan reverted to his earlier questions. "Just to clarify, did we establish that you're in interior design or—"

"Uh-huh." Interior design sounded like a far more sophisticated profession than computer nerd, even if it was absurdly out of character. "Interior designer. That's me," she said wistfully.

"You like what you do?"

She took a chilled bottle from him, nodding. "It might not be everyone's cup of tea, but yeah. I started out helping friends like Natalie, and word of mouth spread. I size up new clients, try to understand how they see themselves and how they want others to see them. Then I figure out the best way to capture them visually, to help them present that image." She put a lot of thought into which fonts, graphics, color schemes and page layouts conveyed the most effective mood and brand.

"You must really be a people person to have that kind of insight into strangers and help them express themselves."

A people person? "I never thought of it that way. Of course, this is Mistletoe. There aren't that many true 'strangers.'"

"So you did stay local, then."

"Yes." Thinking of Jane's memorial service—all the things her vivacious aunt had done with her life and all the things Chloe had not—she added emphatically, "But I have plans to travel. Big plans!"

He chuckled. "You don't have to convince me. I believe you."

You shouldn't. Half of what had come out of her mouth tonight was big fat lies. "Dylan…"

"Yes?" His voice slid down her spine, full of promise.

She shivered, whatever she'd been about to say evaporating.

Fresh air, that's what she needed. Fresh air and an enormous do-over where this evening was concerned.

Chloe nodded toward the sliding-glass door. "Mind if we step out on the balcony while we wait?"

"Great idea." He opened the door for them, and a pleasant breeze rippled into the room.

It was a beautiful spring evening, the night soft against Chloe's bare arms, but the balcony itself was incredibly small. She hadn't realized when she suggested coming out here that it would force her and Dylan even closer— not that she was complaining exactly. The heretofore undiscovered brazen part of her wanted to lean into him.

"Pretty night," Dylan murmured, his profile to her. He glanced at the stars, then out at a landscape she imagined was worlds homier than Atlanta. "Nice view, too…even if we are only five stories up instead of looking down from one of the many penthouses to which I am accustomed."

Chloe smirked. "You're mocking me."

He turned. "Maybe just a little."

Smoothing a hand over her hair, he tucked a few strands behind her ear, out of reach of the light wind. His hand rested against her cheek. They stood motionless, so still that Chloe doubted she was even breathing. If asthma attacks felt like *this,* she wouldn't mind them so much. What was oxygen compared to a moment like this, staring into those amazing deep green eyes and seeing herself—a more exotic, more sensual version of herself—reflected?

A mere week ago, she'd been chiding herself at Jane's memorial service to start seizing the day, to take risks and reap the rewards. Now here she was, practically in the arms of the most alluring man she'd ever known. All it would take was a step forward… She stretched up to press her lips to his, although she might have lost her nerve if he hadn't leaned down to meet her.

After one stunned second of paralysis, she closed her eyes and gave herself up to the moment, the once-in-a-lifetime chance to live out cherished fantasies. Wrapping her hand around his neck, she stood on tiptoe and kissed him back, dizzy with sensation.

Carpe Dylan.

Chapter Five

In the past, Dylan had prided himself on having finesse and being in control, but now he found himself reacting with pure instinct and enthusiastic need. C.J. tasted like woman and chocolate and wine, addictive, her mouth smothering his soft groan. It was the kind of kiss a man wanted to crawl inside, losing himself. Everything that had been eating at him lately, all his doubts and frustration, melted away.

Dropping one hand to her waist, he threaded the other through her hair, tilting her head back and deepening the kiss. But he was restless, craving more of the tantalizing contact, not content to keep his hands still when there was so much of her waiting to be explored. He skimmed over the smooth warmth of her shoulders, curving up to the straps of her red dress, letting his fingers slide slightly beneath the fabric. He heard her breath hitch and pulled away slightly.

"Let's go back in," he said with an involuntary glance at the king-size bed just beyond.

"'Kay." She looked shell-shocked, in an adorably

feminine way, her bourbon eyes dazed and her lips swollen.

"You taste like chocolate," he heard himself say, a bit dazed himself.

She raised a finger to her bottom lip. "It's my gloss."

Which he'd no doubt kissed off of her by now—or would in the immediate future. Grinning, he reached for her again.

They were interrupted by a rap on the door and a cheerful male voice calling, "Room service!"

Dylan groaned. The intrusion was his own damn fault—after all, he'd been the one to order the food— but right now the only thing he hungered for was C.J.

She, however, had sprung back at the sound of the knock, guilt stamped all over her features as if she and Dylan were Mistletoe High students again, caught by the principal making out. Would it make her feel self-conscious if Dylan hollered out just to leave the food in the hall?

With a sigh, he opened the door. A guy in a dark suit and his very early twenties was beaming behind a silver cart. "Mr. Echols? It's an honor to meet you, sir. Several of us flipped a coin to see who'd get to bring up your dinner."

Dylan managed not to grimace at the *sir,* feeling much older than the hotel employee even though they were probably only separated by half a dozen years. "Well, it's nice to meet you, too—?"

"Artie. My brother plays catcher over at the school. I made the team when I was there, but mostly warmed the bench. We think he could go all the way. Pro, like you." At Dylan's polite but cool nod, Artie stopped gushing. "Um…where would you like the food, sir?"

As Dylan turned to indicate the table and two chairs, he realized that C.J. had disappeared—into the restroom, he suspected, to freshen her lipstick and smooth her mussed hair.

"Over here is fine," Dylan said, signing for their dinner. "Tell your brother I said good luck."

Artie's youthful grin flashed again. "Will do. Thanks, Mr. Echols!"

It wasn't that Dylan was completely bitter about baseball—he still loved the game and always would—but it continued to sting when people referenced *his* baseball career. His dream had been to be remembered as truly great at the game, and now there was no way of ever knowing how close he could have come.

The creak of the bathroom door was a welcome distraction. C.J. stepped back into the room, and as he'd anticipated, she looked more composed. Except for her eyes. They shimmered with barely banked panic.

"Hungry?" he asked her, gesturing toward the food.

She clutched her purse tightly. "A-actually, I have to go."

"Now? But the food just… Is something wrong?"

"I'm sorry." She hurried toward the door, slowing only long enough to thrust a twenty-dollar bill at him. He was so startled by her exit that he took the money automatically.

"Candy, wait."

She flinched. "I can't." Then she hurried out into the hall.

His impulse was to go after her, find out what had prompted her to flee and try to change her mind, but it seemed unchivalrous to pursue a woman so adamant about leaving.

Bemused, he returned to their dinners and slumped into a chair, thinking that it was a whole lot of food for one man with a dwindling appetite. Intriguing woman, C.J. Beautiful, seemingly successful, funny when she wasn't rigid with anxiety. But she definitely gave some mixed signals. One moment they'd been hot and heavy—

Had he been too aggressive, the way he'd kissed her as if he couldn't get enough of her? *Echols, you ass.* She'd admitted earlier that she was a bit nervous, spending the evening with a former crush, had even blushed sitting right here in this chair. And what had he done? Practically fallen on her like a ravenous beast or, worse, a horny teenage boy.

In a lot of ways, Mistletoe was a quaint, old-fashioned place and C.J. was a local girl. She wasn't a baseball groupie who'd picked him up in a bar or a jaded sophisticate like Heidi. Instead of lobbing her a nice, simple practice ball, he'd brought the heat, scaring off the most promising thing that had happened to him in weeks.

"I AM A BAD PERSON," Chloe told her reflection in the mirrored elevator panels. She pressed her hands to her hot cheeks, trying to figure out what the devil she'd been thinking. *You weren't.* Her brain had short-circuited as soon as she'd seen Dylan down in the lobby. That was the only explanation for everything that had transpired.

She'd wanted so badly to kiss him, to take the chance

she knew she'd never be given again, but it had quickly spiraled out of control, leaving her feeling shaken and inexperienced. *So that's what lust feels like.* With a shiver, she recalled his gentle tug at the straps of her dress, the rasp of his callused fingers against her skin. It was all too easy to imagine those fingers sliding down the bodice of the dress, exploring her. Chloe Malcolm was not the kind of woman who went to a man's hotel room after a few minutes of conversation and let him feel her up!

Especially when she'd *lied* to the man in question. She'd let him think she was a cheerleader, for crying out loud! And a decorator? When he'd called her Candy as she made her escape, she'd wanted to throw up from guilt.

Once she stepped off the elevator, she hurried toward the front of the hotel to catch a cab. She'd text Nat on the way home to let her know so her friend didn't worry. Something casual like "Tired, think I'll turn in early," rather than admit that she was fleeing into the night like the proverbial Cinderella at the stroke of twelve. *Thank heavens for room service.*

If not for the interruption that had broken the sensual spell, would Chloe even now be in the arms of a man calling out another woman's name?

THOUGH DYLAN MADE a halfhearted stab at eating, he conceded defeat pretty soon and placed the tray in the hall for pickup. He flipped on the television to check scores, but nothing held his interest. Sitting on the bed only reminded him of what he'd rather be doing. *Which is probably why she took off. Get your hormones under control.* Had she left the hotel, or had she gone to their reunion after all?

It wasn't a bad idea, he decided. He was restless, alone in the small room. Why not go downstairs, attend the party as originally planned?

In the back of his mind was the thought that perhaps he'd see her there, that he could apologize if he'd offended her with his amorous enthusiasm and maybe even convince her that it would be safe to go out to eat with him tomorrow. Trying to pretend he didn't have ulterior motives, Dylan quickly showered. Then he changed into black slacks and a matching coat over a white button-down shirt, open at the collar. A lot spiffier than his earlier jeans and shirt, although C.J. hadn't seemed to mind his attire. When he hit the button for the elevator, he possessed far more zeal for this reunion than he had when he'd entered the hotel a couple of hours ago.

He passed through the lobby and went downstairs, following the thumping bass of a band. A folding table sat outside a ballroom door, and two women sat chatting with partygoers and checking in late arrivals. One of the ladies working the door was Lilah Baum—he never forgot a pretty redhead—who'd dated the same varsity football player all through high school. Next to Lilah was a dark-haired woman who'd outdressed everyone else in a one-shouldered sparkling white dress.

As he approached, the brunette glanced up from the clipboard in front of her, her mouth curving into a feline smile when she spotted him. "Why, Dylan Echols. I heard rumors you were coming. I'm sure I speak on behalf of the entire female student body when I say we're glad to see you."

Candy Beemis.

She looked almost exactly the same, but even if she hadn't, he would have recognized the drawl. It was like syrup when she was flirting, but it quickly developed a razor's edge if you were fool enough to displease her— the entire baseball team had overheard her dump Nick Zeth, alternately laughing at her colorful word choices and wincing on their teammate's behalf. Until Dylan had seen her just this second, he hadn't remembered much about her other than her being a dark-haired cheerleader. The vague past hadn't been nearly as compelling as the present with a beautiful lady in red. Now that he'd laid eyes on Candy, details about her rushed back. One thing remained wildly unclear, though.

If this was Candy, who the hell had he been kissing upstairs?

"Candy. Long time, no see." *Happen to know anyone running around the hotel impersonating you?*

She fluttered her lashes. "You remember me. I'm flattered."

"Surprised you're not in there being the life of the party," he said lightly, resisting the urge to storm into the ballroom and get answers from a certain mystery woman.

"The volunteers are working in shifts," she explained. "Mine will be over in about fifteen minutes. Look for me inside, and I'll check to see if there's any room left on my dance card."

He smiled noncommittally. "Hey, weird question for you. By any chance, are you an interior decorator?"

She laughed. "No, why? Is this leading to some cheesy line about how I beautify my surroundings?"

"Sorry." He shook his head. "Must have you confused with someone else. Did we go to school with another Candy? Who was also a cheerleader with dark hair?" In a high school as small as theirs? That was so statistically unlikely that he felt ridiculous just asking.

"No. I'm a one and only," she said with an indignant toss of her hair.

"Right." People were now standing in line behind him. He should go, but he took one last futile stab. "You don't happen to remember a girl we went to school with named C.J., do you?"

Candy narrowed her eyes. "What's with you? Get beaned one too many times in the head with the baseball?"

Lilah Baum—who was probably no longer Baum, judging from the ring on her left hand—was much kinder but no further help. "We had a linebacker named J. C. Delgorio," she told him, "but I don't remember any C.J., male or female."

"Thanks," he said weakly, officially feeling stupid. A distantly familiar and much-loathed sensation.

With Candy glaring after him—apparently it was bad form to be obsessed with some lesser brunette when she'd offered *her* dance card—he slunk through the doors to the ballroom. Except for the bright stage spotlights, the lighting was dim. Dylan paused, letting his eyes adjust, and scanned the crowd for flashes of telltale red. *When I get my hands on her...*

Wrong line of thought. He hardened at the memory of how she'd felt in his hands.

Okay, no touching this time. But "C.J." definitely owed him an explanation. After a purposeful circuit of the room, he was forced to conclude she wasn't there. Natalie was, though. The blonde danced with a tall man Dylan didn't remember. As the song ended, he started toward them. Natalie could give him answers, but he didn't get anywhere near her.

"Echols!"

Nick Zeth, known in years past as Z-Man, and former outfielder Shane McIntyre intercepted him. Shane had on a suit and tie; Nick had opted to pair his old baseball jersey with black slacks. Both men wore name tags that featured yearbook photos. Dylan found that he was suddenly a rabid supporter of name tags; people should be required to wear them at all times. *Especially enigmatic brunettes with identity crises.*

The guys insisted he have a drink with them. They grabbed a couple of beers and sat at a table far enough away from the speakers to have a normal conversation. Shane said he'd caught one of Dylan's broadcasts when he was in Atlanta on business, and Nick, now a local firefighter, revealed that he'd divorced his college sweetheart last year, although he seemed more rueful than bitter. Eventually talk turned to Coach Burton's retirement dinner, which they were all attending.

"He was the best," Shane said.

"He was like a dad to me," Nick reminisced. His own father, also a fireman, had died rescuing a civilian when Nick was in middle school.

It seemed wrong for Dylan to add that Coach B. had

been like a dad to him, too, since Michael Echols had been alive.

"Everything okay, man?" Shane nudged his arm. "You keep looking around the room."

"Looking for a woman," he admitted.

Nick grinned. "Dude, they're nothing but trouble. You're better off with us."

"Not my type." Dylan grinned back.

"You still got a thing for redheads?" Shane wanted to know.

"This one was brunette. But she *was* wearing a red dress."

"Oh, so you're not just looking, you've already found one?" Nick scanned the crowd curiously.

"She temporarily got away," Dylan said. "I'm trying to figure out who she was."

"You could always check the table over there," Shane suggested. "Where the name tags are? Someone on the reunion committee put together a book, a 'where are they now' thing that has pictures and info about everyone."

Dylan got to his feet. "Great. You guys don't mind if I…?"

"Nah." Shane waved his hand. "I was thinking about asking someone to dance. You're not my type, either."

"We'll catch up with you at the coach's banquet if not tonight," Nick said. "Go get her, bro."

There were only a few unclaimed name tags on the long table, Dylan's among them. He winced at the picture of himself, the cocky smile that said he knew what his ticket out of here was and that he was off to bigger and better things. Far away from the struggles he hadn't liked people to see and, more important, away from Michael Echols. *And here I am, back again.* Dylan shoved the tag into his coat pocket and studied the remaining female faces on the table.

Chloe Ann Malcolm? Her middle name wasn't even Jane!

Squinting, he double-checked, comparing the wide-eyed teenager in black and white to the temptress who'd kissed him on the balcony. Not the best picture, but that was her, all right. Chloe Malcolm. He couldn't remember anything about her, but his recollections were probably clouded by his time with her tonight.

On the corner of the table was the green binder Shane had mentioned. Someone had printed out a label and stuck it on the front: *Mistletoe High, Class of 1999.* He flipped through the alphabetical entries until he located Chloe. Background information included her graduating with honors, top ten of their class and her superstar status in Academic Decathlon. Since high school, she'd gone to college, where she earned a degree in computer science. She'd ultimately settled in Mistletoe, near her parents, and ran her own business building and maintaining Web sites.

Dylan ground his teeth. She was a braniac, one of those people who'd effortlessly earned A's when he'd struggled for C's. What had possessed her to tell him she was a cheerleader and an interior decorator? Instead of correcting his mistaken impression that she was Candy, she was having a laugh at the dumb jock's expense.

He must really be dumb. Co-worker Liza Finnell

was attracted to him, but *she* didn't cause even a blip on his radar. If he had half a brain, he'd ask out the sweet, easy-to-read woman. Instead he'd been drawn to Heidi, who'd used him as a rung on her social-climbing ladder but had at least been honest about the basics—say, her *name*. Then he'd spent tonight flirting with a woman who didn't respect him enough even to tell him who she was. Everything his old man had ever said about his lack of intelligence circled through Dylan's mind like a cruel wind. He had noticed inconsistencies in the way Chloe was behaving tonight, but he'd never once dreamed that she might be flat-out lying to him.

It was the second time in a month he'd been left looking like a fool because of a duplicitous female. Before he left Mistletoe, he and Ms. Malcolm were going to have a chat.

THE PHONE RANG at such an unholy hour of the morning that it certainly would have wakened Chloe if she'd actually been able to sleep. She'd gotten tired of staring at the dark ceiling overhead sometime between three and four, tromping in her robe and bare feet to the computer. Might as well get some work done, she'd reasoned. But her mind had been too preoccupied with replaying each second with Dylan—particularly the kissing—to focus on database fields.

"Hello?" As she answered, she experienced a frisson of irrational fear that it would somehow be Dylan on the other end.

Thank heavens it was Natalie instead. "Hey! You took off way too early last night. You had to know I would call first thing for details. What happened that sent you sneaking away without a goodbye?"

Chloe could insist that she hadn't been "sneaking," that she'd merely wanted to get home and knew Nat was busy with her reunion responsibilities, but this was her best friend. "I screwed up. You never should have left me alone with Dylan! I was a mess."

"You've always been more critical of yourself than anyone else is. Candy notwithstanding," Natalie conceded. "Even if you stammered or put your foot in your mouth, I'm sure he didn't find it as noticeable as you did."

"He thought I *was* Candy."

"Huh?" Nat sounded appropriately flummoxed. In what parallel universe could Chloe be mistaken for head cheerleader and budding socialite Candy Beemis?

"Maybe it was seeing me with you that threw him, but he honestly thought I was Candy. And I…sort of let him go on believing that. I told him to call me C.J., and that I work as an interior designer."

There was a strangled sound that was either laughter or a gasp. "You're kidding me!"

"Oh, how I wish I were."

"So…the two of you talked for a little while, under false pretenses, and you felt so bad about it that you went home?"

"Close. We went up to his hotel room, made out for a while under false pretenses and then when room service interrupted with our dinner, I beat a hasty retreat before I ended up sleeping with him or telling him some other incredible whopper like I was once crowned Miss Georgia, right before I invented the Internet."

"You made out with Dylan Echols?" Natalie's voice was full of awe. "You're my heroine."

"*Nat!* Haven't you heard what I've been telling you? I was a disaster. I barely had control of what was coming out of my mouth. He kissed me, then called me Candy."

"Okay, that part would have been a tad ooky. But the rest of it—"

"Natalie, promise you'll never leave me alone with another hot guy."

Her friend's sigh came through loud and clear. "Honey, your life's not going to be terribly interesting if you never spend any alone time with guys."

"I don't want interesting," Chloe resolved. "I wasn't meant for interesting. I tried it last night, and you see how that turned out!"

"You looked stunning and ended up kissing a guy half the women in town have drooled over. Things could have gone worse."

"Not by much. I felt terrible, running out on him like that." She pinched the bridge of her nose, reliving her graceless exit. "He probably thinks I'm off my meds."

This time, the noise Natalie made was definitely a laugh. "If it's any consolation, it's *Candy* he thinks is nuts, not you."

"And yet I don't feel comforted by that. The only thing I find comforting about this whole mess is that he's probably packing up to leave town by now."

"No way he would miss Coach B.'s dinner tomorrow," Natalie interjected. "I think he's even giving a speech or something."

"Right. I forgot about that." Even someone as far removed from athletics as Chloe knew about Coach Todd Burton—he was a town institution. Her heart sank. "Wait, do you think Candy will be there?" The last thing Chloe needed was for Dylan to run into Candy.

"Nah. There's no love lost between her and the coach. He bawled her out once when she dated two baseball players at once, pitting them against each other. She retaliated by whining to her friends that the coach gets too much credit when it's the guys on the field winning the games."

So Coach and Candy didn't get along? Chloe was surprised then that Dylan would cheerfully seek out the former cheerleader. Or maybe, after all he'd been through professionally and personally, he didn't recall petty squabbles from a decade ago.

She regrouped. "All right, so he's in town for at least another day or so. But eventually—*soon*—he will leave. Given his track record for staying away from Mistletoe, I won't ever have to worry about seeing him again." More important, she wouldn't have to dwell on her own asinine behavior.

"At least not until the twentieth reunion," Natalie teased.

"I'm busy that weekend," Chloe said flatly. She was done with high school reunions. She was also finished with wine. *In vino veritas, my butt.* After a minute passed, she stopped obsessing over her own evening long enough to ask, "Tell me *you* had a good time last night?" Natalie deserved to have fun after all the work she'd put into the event.

"I did, thanks." Natalie sighed. "I'm just sorry you didn't get more out of it."

The memory of Dylan's kiss tingled through her, and she pressed a hand to her lips. "It was… I have a lot of work to do. Call you later?"

"You busy tonight? I can bring over comfort food and a couple of chick flicks and get my shoes back."

Chloe knew "comfort food" meant chicken-fried steak and made-from-scratch mashed potatoes from the Dixieland Diner, both topped with white pepper gravy. She was powerless to resist. *Good thing I own that treadmill.* "Sounds like just what the doctor ordered, thanks."

After they disconnected, Chloe once again looked at her computer monitor, but lacked the mental energy to pretend she was getting anything done. Instead, she did seven and a half miles on the treadmill, then jumped in the shower. By the time she got out, she'd worked up an actual appetite. She padded to the fridge in a pair of denim shorts and a purple shirt printed with flowers that spelled out GET LEI'D IN MAUI. A gift from Aunt Jane, naturally. It was the least risqué of the bawdy T-shirts, acceptable Saturday wear for bumming around the house.

A quick scan of the shelves reminded her that, with everything else that had happened this week, she'd neglected grocery shopping. Maybe getting out of the house would help her get out of her head, too, putting last night's absurdities behind her. She would certainly be more productive at the market than she had been at her computer.

She grabbed her car keys and was parking near Mistletoe's only big grocery store fifteen minutes later.

Making a mental list of items she needed, she headed up the sidewalk into the shop. Since Nat was coming over tonight, ice cream was a must-have, but she'd save that for the end of her trip, so it didn't all melt in the cart. Instead, she rounded the corner toward the produce section and stopped cold at the sight of Dylan Echols examining fresh oranges.

Eek.

Well, who needed fruits and vegetables, anyway? She could live without them for another few days. Executing a stealthy about-face, she retreated to the soft-drink aisle, grabbing several things at random before continuing to speed away, wanting to put as much floor space as possible between her and Dylan. With little more in her cart than lunch for today and ice cream for tonight, she checked out, breathing a sigh of relief as she swiped her debit card. As soon as the kid at the register handed her the receipt, she'd be home fr—

"C.J.?"

Oh God. This was karmic punishment for her dishonesty last night.

Did she dare ignore him? If so, he might call out louder and create a scene. It was in her best interest to get their encounter over quietly—and *quickly*. Trapped, she turned with a weak wave as Dylan closed the distance between them. A smiling middle-aged woman stepped aside so that he could get in line behind Chloe.

If anything, he looked even better this morning, in a close-fitting T-shirt that did amazing things for his biceps. And he was making the most of the unshaven look that worked so well on some guys, lending a rugged touch.

Chloe was at a loss for what to say. "Hey." Even that monosyllable strained her current capabilities.

For an instant, Dylan's expression was inscrutable. Then he gave her a grin so wolfish she almost felt the top of her head to check for a red hood. "It *is* you. Must be my lucky day."

Chapter Six

Dylan wanted to pump his fist in the air and let out a whoop of victory. He couldn't have asked for a better moment than this, his beautiful liar of last night caught off guard, her eyes wide and stricken. When he'd read her bio at the reunion, he'd been furious and imagined a straightforward confrontation, asking her point-blank about her identity and watching her squirm over the inevitable truth. But some imp took hold of him as he studied her. With all her hair skimmed back in a high ponytail and wearing practically no makeup, she looked as fresh faced and innocent as she probably had in her teens.

It incensed him anew that a woman who would knowingly make a fool out of him looked so damn much like a schoolgirl. Only her colorful shirt—*get lei'd?*—and shiny full lips hinted at possible naughtiness. He was annoyed to find himself wondering if she once again tasted like chocolate.

"I was sorry you had to leave in such a rush last night," he said, trying to forget how hopeful he'd been about seeing her in the ballroom. And how terrible he'd felt for possibly scaring her off with overzealous ardor. Idiot. He managed not to grit his teeth. "I hope it wasn't anything I did?"

"N-no. Nothing like that. I had somewhere I needed to be."

"The reunion?" he pressed. "I looked for you downstairs."

She caught her bottom lip between her teeth. "When I was fixing my makeup, I noticed…that I had a text message. From a friend. Needing help."

"I see. Is everything okay?"

"Mmm-hmm. It was just a, um, girl thing. All taken care of now."

The fact that she was a lousy liar made him feel like an even bigger chump for not seeing through her last night. How could he have fallen for anything that came out of her mouth? *Maybe because you were too busy fantasizing about the mouth in question.*

He handed over a twenty that covered the few basics he'd picked up for his mother, then followed Chloe out the door without bothering to wait for his change. No way was he letting her escape before she confessed her perfidy.

"I was sorry we didn't get to talk longer about your job," he said.

"My job?"

He nodded, grinning as a spontaneous plan took shape. "The interior decorating. What's your specialty?" He had no idea whether decorators even *had* specialties.

"Feng sway?" It came out as a tentative squeak. "Shui. Feng shui."

"Because I was thinking of having my condo re-decorated." He wondered how much rope he needed to hand her before she hanged herself.

"B-but you live in Atlanta!"

"Hardly the far corners of the earth." He shrugged. "It's not too bad a drive. Surely not *all* your clients are in Mistletoe? If I hired you, I'd know I wasn't getting ripped off by some stranger in the city. And as an extra bonus, I'd get to see you again."

"No, I—" She broke off, looking even more alarmed than before, if such a thing were possible.

He followed her gaze to a pregnant woman farther down the sidewalk. The spring breeze plastered her blue maternity dress to the small baby bulge, and a headband was keeping the raven-black hair out of her eyes while she took pictures with a digital camera. She seemed to be photographing storefronts.

Turning back to Chloe, he asked, "Someone you know?"

After a brief hesitation, Chloe admitted, "Rachel Waide. But she's working right now. For the chamber of commerce. Very artistic. She hates to be bothered while she's trying to get the perfect shot," she added, already striding in the opposite direction.

Dylan amiably tagged along. "I don't know if you realize this about me, but I'm very stubborn. Coach taught me to hang in there all nine innings and go for the win. I really would like to talk to you more about decorating my place. Or at least coming to look at it before you turn me down completely."

They were passing a woman with what appeared to

be her teenage son, and Chloe ducked her head, clearly hoping not to be recognized by any of her fellow citizens.

"How about I buy you lunch and we can chat?" He aimed his most charming smile directly at her. "Come on, you owe me for running off last night, *C.J.* Is the Dixieland Diner still in business?"

"I can't go out to lunch. My ice cream would melt."

"Dinner, then?" he persisted. "Or why don't you just give me your business card. I'll come by your office later and—"

"I work from home."

"Even better. We can go there and have lunch together. To protect your ice cream," he added with a smile.

She stared back with a deer-in-the-headlights look, finally sighing in resignation. For a moment, he thought she was about to cop to not being an interior decorator. "Fine. Follow me."

Game on, then?

He nodded. "Lead the way." *This should be interesting.*

CHLOE BRIEFLY entertained the fantasy of mashing down the accelerator and not stopping. She'd recently decided she wanted to see more of the world—here was her chance! Yet she was slowly realizing that Dylan Echols wouldn't be that easy to shake. Besides, she only had about a quarter of a tank of gas. As great escapes went, that wouldn't get her far.

Cursing her luck, she stayed right at the legal speed limit, neither too slow nor too fast, and dutifully signaled with her blinker well before each turn. *Story of my life*. Until this weekend, anyway. Dylan stayed close, impossible to miss in her rearview mirror. Even his car was sexy—a recent-model dark metallic-blue Mustang convertible.

Driving around with the top down, he looked like a man without cares. If she hadn't known about his shoulder injury and subsequent career disappointment, she would have bought into the illusion. He seemed to have bounced back well, though. She wondered if he enjoyed his sports reporting job. Addressing a faceless audience with a camera trained on her sounded like purgatory to her. Chloe did better in front of a computer than she did in front of people.

Which made it thoroughly ironic that she was having two meals with Dylan in as many days. Why in heaven's name had she capitulated to his suggestion that he come over for lunch? Well, there had been the fear of being recognized, of course, and her escalating need to end their conversation in front of the store, but that was the logical, intellectual reason. On a purely instinctual level, when a man like Dylan Echols said, "Take me home," a woman's automatic response was *yes!*

When Chloe parked under the carport, he was quick to hop out of his own vehicle and offer a hand with the groceries. She thanked him as she gave him the bag of ice cream.

"What about you?" she asked. "Do you have anything you need to put in the refrigerator?"

He shook his head. "I just grabbed a few things to take over to my mom's this afternoon. Nothing that won't keep for a little while."

That was nice of him; she could identify with taking care of your parents. Not only did Chloe miss Aunt Jane horribly, her passing made Chloe even more conscious of her parents' age.

She swallowed. "How's your mother doing? I mean, I heard that your dad had passed away. That must be hard on her, living alone after so many years of marriage."

He was silent, remote behind the sunglasses he wore. Then he said, "I suppose it is," and strode past her on the sidewalk even though he'd have to wait for her to unlock the front door.

Lesson learned. Apparently, even with the months that had passed, he wasn't ready to talk about his late father.

She climbed the steps to the front porch, thinking back to earlier in the week. It had been such a surprise to find that package from Aunt Jane. How could Chloe have known she was in for a bigger shock—Dylan Echols right here at her door? She ushered him inside, grateful for the tiny bit of redecorating she'd managed since moving into the house. Undecorating, rather.

Chloe was the only child of adoring parents, and the place had looked like a shrine to her. Framed pictures of her entire childhood had filled the wall space in the hallway and trophies from the Academic Decathlon and sophomore science fair had perched on the mantel. Her parents had taken their favorite portraits with them to their smaller apartment, but had left so much of it here that she'd felt a little embarrassed living among the memorabilia her first week back at home.

Was the Echols house a similar museum to Dylan's

achievements? Like her, Dylan was an only child, and she imagined his parents must have been bursting with pride for him. There were probably team pictures, from kindergarten community league to the major leagues, and sports trophies in every room.

"So this is your place, huh?" Sliding off his glasses, Dylan glanced around at the serviceable but worn furniture, her mother's faded floral curtains and the rug Chloe planned to replace with faux hardwood. Eventually.

Dylan raised an eyebrow. "I have to admit, it's not what I expected from a decorator. But then, you're just full of surprises."

Her heart hammered. Surprises as in her kissing him last night, or her fleeing immediately afterward? "Well, you know what they say about the cobbler's children having no shoes? It's like that with decorators, too."

The sensible thing to do would be trying to convince him that she was a lousy decorator so that he'd abandon any half-baked notion of hiring her. But she was already humiliated enough over last night and hated for him to think she was completely incompetent.

She found herself adding, "Besides, I haven't been here long enough to renovate much. It was my parents' place, and they recently gave it to me. Moved into their own apartment at the seniors' center. They're older than a lot of my friends' parents," she explained. Nat's mom had recently hit fifty, but could pass for a woman in her late thirties—good genes in that family.

"These your folks?" Dylan gestured toward a magnetic frame on the refrigerator. In the picture, her mother was wearing a bright green sweater and her dad a suit with a Christmas-tree tie.

Chloe nodded. "Yeah. That was taken at the Winter Wonderland Dance."

"I remember that dance." His smile was nostalgic. "For this town it was like homecoming and prom all rolled into one."

He was right. Even though it seemed more heavily chaperoned than a high school event because of all the adults, the annual charity formal had always been a big deal among her classmates, wondering who would invite whom. Even the strictest of parents normally allowed their children to attend since it was a community fund-raiser, benefiting the seniors' center and adjacent medical complex. No guy had ever asked Chloe, though. Her junior year, Natalie had tried to force a double date with her own date's cousin who was visiting for the holidays, but it had turned out to be such an awkward fiasco that Chloe had skipped the whole thing her senior year, telling her parents she'd rather use the time to study for winter finals.

She didn't realize she was scowling until Dylan asked, "Did I say something wrong?"

"Not at all. Just trying to decide on a plan for lunch. Pizza okay with you?"

"Sure." He stayed out of her way while she bustled around the small kitchen, stowing her newly purchased groceries. "But I still can't believe you opted for manual labor over my buying you lunch at the diner."

"Well, there was the ice cream to consider," she reminded him lamely.

The bigger consideration was the half-dozen people who would have greeted her at the diner, where she was a regular. Just the thought of being exposed as a fraud left her wanting her inhaler. Dylan would be gone again soon. Couldn't she have this small, stolen period of time with him and retain her dignity?

Then say something, she scolded herself, *and stop just standing here with a guilty expression.* She cleared her throat. "Besides, my dinner plans are for the diner."

"Ah. Hot date?"

If it weren't for the faint brackets of tension around his mouth, she would have assumed he was poking fun at her, but she reconsidered from his perspective. If Dylan Echols had deemed her attractive and interesting enough to have dinner with last night, why *wouldn't* she be good enough for some other guy to take to dinner? It was an unfamiliar yet pleasant way to think of herself.

"Just dinner with a friend. Nothing romantic."

His shoulders relaxed almost imperceptibly. "As embarrassing as this is to admit, I think I would have been jealous."

It ranked among the most flattering things a man had ever said to her—right up there with technophobe Zachariah Waide telling her that the Web site she'd created for his supply store was a user-friendly work of art. "Th-thank you."

Dylan's eyes held hers. "You're welcome."

The moment took on an intimacy that heightened both her attraction to him and her discomfort. She turned away to preheat the ancient oven, then got out a baking sheet. When the metal hit the counter, she realized for the first time how quiet her house was. It never bothered her when she was alone, but somehow it seemed even more quiet with him here.

As she threw away the cardboard box and plastic wrapping, he asked, "How'd you get into feng shui?"

"You could say I followed an impulse."

"I've heard of it in passing, but never met anyone who uses it. I'd love to hear some specifics."

Gulp. She'd only mentioned feng shui because, at the time, it had been the single decorating term she could even think of. In retrospect, she should have told him her specialty was commercial interiors. Since there was no way he had the authority to hire her to redecorate a television station, that would have been a tidy way to end the discussion. *I have to get better at thinking on my feet.*

Except what she really meant was that she should get better at lying, a thought that made her queasy. Her parents would be horribly disappointed in her.

"Well, as you probably know, feng shui is an ancient Asian art. Or maybe more like a tradition. A *philosophy*. Having to do with the placement of items in the home and the different ways said placement can affect the home owner."

"Such as?" He took a seat, watching her with fascination.

Chloe wanted to groan. After hearing Nat and other girlfriends complain about dating guys who talked only about themselves, why did *she* have to find such a good listener? Stalling, she opened the refrigerator with vague intentions of pulling together a salad to accompany the pizza. Until she remembered that she'd not bought any produce because she'd been dodging Dylan. *And here he sits in your kitchen. Excellent job with the avoidance, girl genius.*

She straightened. "Are you sure you're really interested in hearing this? It's pretty metaphysical. Probably not your cup of tea."

"Why, because I'm just a jock?"

Oddly, in that moment, he reminded her of Candy Beemis, the way the other woman would say something under the pretext of "just kidding" when, in reality, she was speaking her mind. The difference was that Dylan wasn't targeting someone else with the disparaging humor, but himself. Though his tone was light enough to be considered jesting, there was a vulnerability in his green eyes that sliced straight through Chloe. An insecurity, even.

Had someone made him feel like "just a jock"? He had to know there was more to his personality than that…although maybe he was more sensitive to the issue now that baseball had been ripped out of his life. A knot formed in her chest. On top of her other crimes this weekend, she'd inadvertently belittled him just because she was trying to cover her own butt. After all the times she'd felt inadequate in her life, she couldn't stand to do the same to someone else, even accidentally.

"I'll come to your apartment," she blurted.

Both his eyebrows shot up. "You're kidding."

Well, he couldn't be any more surprised by the spontaneous offer than *she* was.

"You caught me unawares today—I don't usually give presentations to former crushes while standing in my kitchen in bright purple T-shirts of dubious taste— but I'll get my materials together and do a formal consultation for you later in the week." *After* she'd had time to learn something about feng shui but *before* she lost her nerve. Unless… "I'm afraid it will have to be soon. Starting next month, my schedule just takes off. But if you don't have the time right now, I under—"

"Not a problem."

"Oh. Great," she lied. *This is getting to be a bad habit.*

She wanted to smack her forehead and just admit all; it seemed simpler than continuing this far-fetched charade. But she looked into those green eyes and forgot what she was going to say. As Natalie had grumbled during their teen years, Chloe avoided conflict whenever possible, even if it meant letting someone like Candy occasionally run over her. While Chloe hoped she'd matured past some of that, the thought of the conflict, the *contempt,* she'd cause if she told Dylan the sordid truth made her stomach clench.

Grateful to break eye contact, she put the pizza in the oven and set the timer.

As soon as she sat at the table with him, he asked, "So, you have a home office?"

"Down the hall. But it's way too messy for anyone to see," she prevaricated. Chloe was compulsively neat, a holdover from her mother believing that if they could just keep the home dust-free Chloe wouldn't have asthma attacks. Rose had kept the house meticulous and raised Chloe to do the same.

"Fair enough. But do you have a portfolio of your work here that you show perspective clients?"

"Actually, no. That's a good idea, though."

"Surely you have a Web site."

"It's, um, down temporarily. Being transitioned to a new server." She bounced out of her chair like a demented jack-in-the-box. "I'm being a terrible hostess. Can I get you a drink?"

"Whatever you're having."

Her hands trembled as she pulled a jug from the fridge. Dylan sat looking so relaxed in comparison that she wanted to scream just to relieve some of her tension.

He smiled. "For the record, I like the bright purple shirt. Have you actually been lei'd?"

Lemonade sloshed over the top of the pitcher. "Excuse me?"

He flashed that same wolfish smile from this morning. "What I mean is, have you been to Hawaii? You mentioned wanting to travel. I wondered if the shirt was a personal souvenir or a gift from someone else or…"

"Ah." Barely paying attention to what she was doing, she tore too many paper towels off the roll to clean up her spill. "Gift. From my late aunt Jane. She was really something…visited at least four continents. She sent me all kinds of crazy things. She died on her most recent trip. In her sleep, in the Caribbean. There are definitely worse ways to go, so I should be glad."

Dylan studied her, the playfulness gone from his tone. "You miss her."

"A lot. Even though she wasn't in Mistletoe much,

she was still a major presence in my life." She blinked hard against the tears she hadn't expected. "We just buried her last week. To tell you the truth, I haven't been myself ever since. I…"

"Yes?" There was empathy in his voice. Because of how much he missed his father?

Chloe leaned against the counter, staring into the eyes of a man she hadn't seen in ten years, a man who hadn't even known she existed ten years ago. Yet she felt she could tell him anything. Would he understand how she'd so desperately wanted to become the person Aunt Jane saw in her? Chloe knew that her aunt had loved her, had been proud of her, but she was also aware that Jane had hoped for more for her niece. Recently Chloe found herself yearning for an unde- fined *more*…but not enough to change a carefully or- ganized and mostly satisfactory existence to reach for it. At least, not until last night.

That had been a big enough shake to register on the Richter scale. She probably should have hurried for the nearest doorway as soon as she'd seen Dylan in the lobby.

"C.J.?" His tone was heartbreakingly gentle. "Was there something you wanted to say?"

But she didn't think she'd be able to get the words past the lump of emotion. It was all tangled together, and the minute she tried to explain any of it, she'd start sobbing. Her eyes were already stinging. She had plenty to regret about her behavior this weekend, and she wasn't going to add to the list by bursting into tears in front of Dylan.

So she swallowed, reaching for the timer before it had a chance to buzz. "I think the pizza's ready."

"Right." He looked away, and the startling connection between them was broken.

Chloe didn't know whether to be disappointed or relieved.

CHICKEN-FRIED STEAK wasn't nearly as good when it was cold, Chloe discovered. The gravy had congealed unappetizingly while she filled Natalie in on the details of the past twenty-four hours. Natalie, sitting on the living room floor on the opposite side of the rectangular coffee table, had finished her dinner, almost choking on laughter and mashed potatoes when Chloe repeated her supposed specialty.

"Feng shui?" Natalie had sputtered. "What on earth possessed you to say that?"

"It's not like I have an extensive mental encyclopedia of decorating terms to choose from! Heck, I'm lucky I was able to come up with that on the spot. It was just…everyone in this town sees me as a computer geek, which I am, but it was nice for Dylan to see me as—" A total fake? Yeah, much better.

Chloe pushed away her take-out container of untouched food and considered her rash promise. "I can't believe I agreed to go to his apartment." He'd just looked so irresistibly vulnerable. She would have agreed to virtually anything in the moment.

"What I cannot believe is that you've scored more alone time with Dylan Echols." Natalie wagged her brows. "Lucky girl."

"Alone time is how I got into this mess in the first place." Chloe sighed, resting her head against the couch behind her. "Maybe it's not too late to… Think I could convince him that every graduating class has a senior prank and this was it, ten years later?"

"We did have a senior prank. Back in '99. A few guys from the swim team and a few from the chess club took apart the lavatory stalls and reassembled them on the front lawn."

Only partly listening, Chloe tried to regroup. It was devastating to imagine telling Dylan she was a big fat fake. How could she admit that after the way she'd once idolized him, after the immensely flattering way he looked at her? The way he—her skin flushed with warmth—kissed her. She'd officially gotten herself in too deep to undo all the fibs, including the comparatively innocuous one that she had dinner plans with her parents tomorrow. Before he'd left today, Dylan had invited her to be his last-minute date to the dinner honoring the coach.

Stupid irony. The guy of her dreams was seeking her out at seemingly every opportunity, and she had to turn him down because of her own self-sabotage.

Her intellect argued that he was seeking her out for local weekend events because he happened to be here in Mistletoe and she was convenient. Even then, he probably would have rapidly lost interest if she'd said, "Don't you remember? I'm Chloe, the mousy tongue-tied girl you ignored throughout high school. I stayed in Mistletoe, live in my parents' house and work with computers." Where was the glamour and sex appeal in that? Most people were not turned on by HTML code.

"I think I want to be someone else," Chloe said.

"Okay, but *Candy?*" Natalie pulled a face.

"No, not her. Someone with her confidence maybe, but not her cruel streak. Someone who knows how to talk to men. Someone who, when she notices a guy staring, assumes it's for a good reason and not because she tucked her dress into her panty hose. Maybe I shouldn't have stayed in Mistletoe." Chloe was an arguably successful adult; would she have fared better if she'd started fresh someplace, where no one knew her as the wheezy kid or uncoordinated teen?

"Hey!" Natalie looked genuinely alarmed. "I, for one, am thrilled that you stayed in Mistletoe. Don't move!"

"I won't. I was just thinking out loud." Her parents would be crushed if she abandoned them. She knew she couldn't do that.

Natalie shook her head. "I can't believe one stupid reunion has you second-guessing your entire life. It was just a dance, Chloe."

"It isn't only the reunion—it's me. Even before Aunt Jane died, I... Knowing you want to make changes doesn't mean you know where to start. It's scary. And it's difficult to re-create who you are in a place where everyone's known you since preschool. I think, subconsciously, that's why I told Dylan that my name is C.J. and I'm an interior designer. He *doesn't* know me. It was my big chance."

Natalie looked thoughtful, refraining from judgment. "Well, C.J., what are you going to do now?"

"Exactly what I told him I would. Go to his place on Wednesday." She took a deep breath, reminding herself that she'd always been a quick study. With facts and books, anyway, if not people. "I can do this."

"Do what?" Natalie's blue eyes widened. "Decorate his place?"

"No, it won't come to that. I'll quote him a ridiculous price or suggest we do everything in orange and pink feathers or something. He won't hire me. All I need is enough information to bluff my way through a conversation at his apartment. I'll look up some decorating terminology online, maybe get one of those ubiquitous and insultingly titled books. You know the type. *Feng Shui for Fools, Danish Modern for Dumbasses.*"

Natalie snorted. "Now there's the Chloe I love. You have a delightfully dry wit when you're not censoring yourself. I get antsy on bad dates, eager to recap them for you because I know your observations will be more entertaining than the date itself. You can be wicked when you want to."

"Thank you. I think. Jane was like that, unafraid to speak her mind even if it shocked people around her. And it *always* shocked Mama. Funny, you'd think she would have gotten used to it after all those years."

"Chloe." Natalie hesitated, which was so unlike her that it made Chloe sit up and pay closer attention.

"What is it?"

"Don't take this the wrong way, but your parents? They could be really protective. I know you were sick a lot when you were a kid, but that was a long time ago. Don't let their good intentions smother you. You don't have to be perfect for them."

"Last night, I went up to a hotel room with a guy I

barely know and I'm losing count of the lies I've told him. I don't think we need to worry about me being perfect."

"I just meant—"

"I know what you meant." Chloe just wasn't sure how she felt about it. Her parents had tried to do right by her, and she loved them a lot. But she had to admit, there had been times she'd chafed under their sheltering strictures.

Natalie stood. "Come on, then."

"Ice cream time?"

"No, let's hit the Web and see what we can find out about feng shui."

"I hate that you're helping," Chloe said. "I feel like I've made you an accessory, like I'm taking you down with me."

Natalie waved a hand. "Are you kidding? This is exciting stuff. Besides, you know I'd help with anything in my power. I owe you. You're the only reason a bubble brain like me passed math."

"You're not bubble brained!" Chloe protested vehemently.

"Math sure made me feel like I was. Until I met you."

"You just had some bad teachers." Though Chloe herself had never had trouble in school, she knew that some instructors weren't flexible enough to account for different learning styles. "Look at you now! Taking care of the books for a profitable retail operation. You rock."

"Back atcha," Natalie said with a smile. "I was serious about helping you. If you want to make changes, I'm happy to lend advice. Or shoes. Or alibis."

Chloe laughed. The fact that the person who knew her best thought she might need an alibi showed that, for better or worse, Chloe was changing already. *Here goes nothing.*

Chapter Seven

"You're such a good son," Barb Echols said from the hallway.

No, he wasn't. Finished in the closet, Dylan descended the ladder, thinking that his afternoon sounded like the beginning of a joke. *How many ex-baseball players* does *it take to screw in a lightbulb?*

Just one, but it took him months to get around to the job. They both knew he'd done the bare familial minimum for years—mailing tickets to games and the occasional Mother's Day card—but it was just like Barb to content herself on scraps of affection. He'd watched her settle throughout her marriage; an ugly thought chilled him. Was he no better than his father?

"Hey, Mom?" Dylan folded the collapsible ladder and shoved it to the back of the closet, wishing it were as easy to push aside his burgeoning self-disgust. "Would you like to go with me to dinner tomorrow night?"

She blinked the green eyes that he'd inherited. "But you have that important banquet at the KC Hall."

"I know. I'm asking you to come with me as my date."

"Me?" She looked shocked by the small gesture.

Why shouldn't she be? He hadn't even come home for the holidays, citing his busy new work schedule covering college football games. He hadn't known then that it would be his father's last Christmas. *Would I have done anything differently?* He wasn't honestly sure, but his relationship with the man was now a moot point. His mom was a different story.

"Come with me," he reiterated. "Unless you have other plans already? A lady scolded me just earlier today that it's bad manners to ask at the last minute."

Chloe had tried to sound mock-indignant at his eleventh-hour invitation, but he could tell she'd been anxious about the idea of going somewhere in public with him. Still, she'd exhibited plenty of nerve when, instead of wisely backing down, she'd brazenly agreed to come to his condo for a decorating consultation! As if he wouldn't be able to tell she was a fake. What kind of moron did she think he was, to be duped by sputtered nonsense like "a philosophy of the placement of stuff"?

Please. A layman could pick up better specifics than that during a thirty-second HGTV commercial. Chloe was playing him for a fool, but she couldn't keep it up forever.

"Earlier today?" Barb echoed, pursing her lips. "I'm not the first person you've invited to this dinner, am I?"

Oh, hell. Sensitivity was not his strong suit. "Sorry, Mom, I—"

"Are you kidding?" She beamed. "I'd love you to start dating a nice Mistletoe girl!"

She's not that nice. Despite himself, he recalled the self-deprecating way she'd admitted to her high school crush on him—had that part been true?—and the pain in her voice when she spoke of the aunt she'd obviously adored. Plus, she'd blushed last night in his hotel room, hardly seeming a jaded woman of wiles. She had her parents' picture displayed on her fridge as proudly as his mother had once hung his kindergarten drawings and, later, his baseball cards. Chloe had even asked how his mother was faring after his dad's death, showing more compassion than Dylan himself, who avoided thinking about home.

The truth was, he didn't know what to make of the woman.

He considered asking his mother if she knew anything about her, but Barb already looked entirely too delighted by the prospect of his seeing a local girl, probably imagining his being around more and chubby-cheeked grandchildren. He didn't want to get her hopes up, especially since his association with Chloe Malcolm was going to be short-lived and would no doubt end badly once he exposed her as the shameless fraud she was.

As soon as Dylan escorted his mom into the hall, his eyes went to Todd Burton, standing amid a throng of well-wishers. Whether the older man was actually stooped with age or Dylan was taller now than he'd been as a high school freshman, Coach B. seemed smaller than he once had, but he was still just as imposing, just as solid. He'd already been losing his red hair when Dylan had played for him; now, only a circle of faded orange and silver remained around his mostly bald head. Dylan was startled to see that the man had gotten rid of the matching mustache. He'd never seen Coach Burton clean shaven before.

The last time the two of them had seen each other was when Dylan had been in the hospital after the first shoulder surgery. Coach had come to visit him. Michael Echols had not.

When Dylan's father had died right after the new year, Coach Burton had been visiting his daughter in Colorado before the school's spring semester started. He'd ordered an arrangement of flowers for the funeral and later visited Barb to tell her he was here if she needed anything. Dylan wondered if his mother had ever taken the man up on his offer. Barb could be borderline passive-aggressive, depending completely on others while constantly fretting that she didn't "want to be a bother." She'd adopted an apologetic attitude with her own husband, instead of grabbing him by the collar, reminding him that she was half of the marriage, too, and demanding his respect.

In spite of himself, Dylan grinned at the mental image. He would have paid damn good money to see tiny Barb, five foot nothing in her stocking feet, give Michael Echols a piece of her mind. Since leaving home, Dylan had avoided timid women as if they were a curse, gravitating instead toward females who did whatever they wanted. Of course, that practice had netted him women like Heidi. There must be a middle ground he was missing.

"Echols!" The coach had looked up from the people talking to him and spotted his one-time protégé. With a quick nod of dismissal to the people surrounding him, he covered ground in the exact manner Dylan remembered. How many times had he seen that purposeful stride as Coach headed out to the pitcher's mound to confer during practice or a game?

Nostalgia bubbled up, forming a lump of emotion in Dylan's chest. Being a guy, he hadn't cried when he lost his major league career—although, dear God, he'd wanted to at times, wondering if it would help him purge any of the frustration, fury and loss—and he hadn't shed a tear over his father's grave. Barb had sobbed enough for both of them, and Dylan had played the part of the stoic son, holding her and thanking everyone who'd come to pay their respects, knowing that many of them were there out of obligation to his mother not affection for Michael. Now, Dylan's vision blurred for just an instant, his eyes stinging.

Then he blinked, and the world righted itself again. "Coach." He clapped the man's shoulder, leaning into it and making it a half hug. "It's good to see you."

"You, too." Coach Burton squeezed him hard, strong as an ox despite his advancing years. Speaking low enough that only Dylan could hear him, he added, "I'm sorry I couldn't get back in time to be here for you in January, son."

Dylan swallowed and nodded.

Coach Burton moved back, turning to Barb. "Mrs. Echols, you're looking as lovely as ever. I'm glad you made him bring you. It's good to see you again."

"I was glad he asked! You've been such a special person to our whole family." A cloud passed over her face. "I'm just sorry Michael couldn't be here for this."

Taking the diplomatic path, Coach patted her arm and said nothing. During his summers off, he'd attended some of Dylan's pro games. They'd gone out for beer afterward once, and Coach Burton had let slip the opinion that any man who routinely made himself feel more important by belittling his kid should be horse-whipped. As Dylan approached thirty, he found himself wondering if he'd ever settle down and if, assuming he ever became a parent himself someday, he'd be a decent dad. After all, his own father hadn't provided a shining role model. *But I had Coach.* That was more than some kids ever got.

Other guys were coming through the doorway now, including Nick and Shane, who was accompanied by a very pretty girl with golden hair. Both men hailed Dylan with loud greetings.

His mother smiled. "You'll be wanting to catch up with old friends. I should get out of your way."

Coach Burton extended his arm gallantly. "You two will sit with me. Can I show you to the head table? Maybe get you a drink?"

Looking ten years younger, Barb nodded.

Shane strolled up, introducing his date. "Dylan, this is Arianne Waide. Ari, Dylan Echols."

She grinned, her eyes twinkling at Dylan. "You went to school with my older brothers. I watched you pitch some great games."

"Waide?" Dylan flashed back to the pregnant photographer yesterday. "Any relation to Rachel?"

The blonde nodded. "She's one of my sisters-in-law. Lilah Waide is the other."

Right, now he remembered the name of Lilah Baum's steady boyfriend throughout high school. Tanner Waide. He'd been a fairly decent football player, but had been far more passionate about Lilah than sports.

"Nice to meet you, Arianne." Smirking at Shane, Dylan leaned closer to her. "You do realize you're too good for this guy here, right?"

She laughed. Shane, less amused, socked Dylan in the shoulder—not the one that had been injured, thank heavens.

"Shane and I are just good buddies," Arianne said. "Honestly, I think he asks me out because he hopes I can get him a discount on fishing equipment at the family store."

"That's not why I ask you out," Shane insisted. "Although now that you mention it…"

Heckling each other, the two of them moved farther into the room, leaving Nick and Dylan behind.

"I didn't want to ask for details in front of Ari," Nick began, "but did you track down your mysterious lady in red the other night?"

"As a matter of fact." Maybe Nick knew more about her. "Chloe Malcolm. Is she—"

"Klutzy Chloe?" Behind them, a man guffawed. "Don't tell me *she's* here tonight. Better keep her away from the punch table."

Next to Dylan, Nick had stiffened. His unsmiling expression fell several degrees cooler than civil. "Petey."

Dylan turned to find Peter "Petey" Grubner holding a drink and sporting the same severe crew cut he'd favored ten years ago, atop a much rounder face. Their former teammate had gained about thirty pounds. What Dylan remembered about the guy was that Petey had often tried too hard to fit in, laughing loudly at his own jokes or picking fights with other teams to prove his "boys" had his back. To give him credit, though, he'd had a decent batting average. One of the best in the county, but he'd lacked the discipline to do anything with his God-given talent.

"Hello, Pete." Even though he'd heard far stranger nicknames in professional sports, Dylan would feel asinine calling another grown man Petey.

"Dylan Echols." The man bared his teeth in a smile. "We're honored that you took time from your high-powered big-city career to hang out with us yokels."

"No chance I'd miss Coach's send-off," Dylan said easily, refusing to be disturbed by someone else's bitterness. *Not when I already have plenty of my own.*

"Shocked no one asked him to retire years ago." Grubner sipped whatever was in his red plastic cup. "I mean, I like the guy as much as the rest of you, but he's been at Mistletoe High ever since it was a one-room schoolhouse for the pioneers' kids. It'll do everyone good to get new blood."

Go away, Grubner. "Who've they got to replace him?" Dylan asked Nick.

"They don't. They're still interviewing. The assistant coach, Asbury, will fill in for the interim, but he's not too far off from retirement himself. They can make him head coach, but then they'll be going through the same process in a couple of years."

Grubner rocked back on his heels, puffing up his

chest. "You know, I thought about going into coaching instead of taking over the car dealership, but it's a good thing I followed in the family footsteps. Coaching just wouldn't be fair to Petey Jr. Wife's home with him tonight 'cause he's got some stomach bug, but he's a strapping boy. Quite the baseball future ahead of him. Why spend all my time and energy on a team that changes every year when I can devote every spare minute to shaping Junior's career?"

Petey Jr. had Dylan's sympathies. "Well, it's been nice catching up, but—"

"When I walked over, you were talking about Chloe Malcolm." Grubner was studying the room with predatory interest. "Where is she?"

"Not here," Dylan said, unintentionally biting off the words. "I ran into her briefly at the reunion."

Again with the braying guffaw—one of Petey's many donkeylike qualities. "She actually showed up? I'm surprised she left her computer long enough to venture out in public. That little gal's scared of her own shadow. Most exciting thing she ever did was douse Candy Beemis in punch at a high school dance." He leered. "Even back then, Candy was an excellent candidate for a wet T-shirt contest."

"She dumped punch on Candy?" Had Dylan stumbled into some bizarre, grudge-match rivalry?

"Not on purpose. Why d'you think we call her Klutzy Chloe? I remember this one time she—"

"Dude." Nick interrupted, rolling his eyes so hard his sockets probably had whiplash. "That was over a decade ago. Grow the hell up."

When Nick stalked off, Dylan and Petey were left staring at each other in surprise. Dylan recovered first, muttering a quick, "I should be going, too."

He caught up with his friend waiting in line at the open bar. "No one could accuse you of mellowing with age." But his tone was openly admiring. Grubner had been working his nerves, too.

Nick looked sheepish. "That guy makes me insane. I didn't like him when we were in school, but he was part of the team. Then he and his wife lived next door to me for a while with these three yappy little dogs. He was the type who complained about everything—say, if a leaf from one of my trees blew into his yard. They moved across town to a bigger place once Petey Jr. outgrew his nursery, and I nearly threw a block party to celebrate."

"How old is the poor kid?"

"Around seven. With all the pressure his dad puts on him, he's probably going to hate sports before he even gets into junior high." Nick asked for two beers, then admitted as they moved away from the bar, "I didn't like how that blowhard was ragging on Chloe."

"So you know Chloe?"

"Not well. You remember my grades slipping junior year? Plummeting, really. That's when Mom started seriously dating again, and I had a tough time dealing with it. You know how strict Coach has always been about no pass, no play. My chem teacher asked Chloe to help me. Nice girl. Maybe a little…awkward, but decent. I see her around town sometimes. She grew up to be a looker, but I'm not sure she knows it."

So far, Dylan had seen her in a low-cut red dress and a flamboyant purple shirt with a suggestive slogan. It wasn't a wardrobe that screamed "shy." Although she definitely had her bashful moments. Hell, maybe she was a split personality. *Chloe and C.J.* Would that make sleeping with her a threesome?

Grimacing at his inappropriately wayward thoughts, Dylan pushed her out of his mind and focused on socializing with other ball players, some from his time at Mistletoe High and others who had come before or since but shared a mutual respect for Coach Burton.

"I brought my mom with me," he told Nick, "and I've ignored her too long. Why don't you come say hi. She'd like that."

"Sure." Having vented on Grubner, Nick was back to his affable self.

Barb was seated between the coach, who'd lost his wife decades ago to breast cancer and later declared himself married to his job, and the Asburys. She looked like she was having the time of her life, so enthusiastic that it made Dylan wonder if she got out of the house enough. Having lived in Mistletoe since birth, she must have enough friends and neighbors to keep her social calendar filled.

Before long, the waitstaff announced that dinner would be served. People who had been mingling in clumps throughout the hall gradually found their way to their seats.

Over the salad course, Coach Burton asked Dylan, "You nervous about giving the speech?"

God, yes. "No. I plan to regale them with stories

about how your answer to everything was 'walk it off.'"
Dylan smiled at Assistant Coach Asbury. "Whereas you
always told us to 'ice it.'"

Coach Burton chortled. "He's got you there, Steve."
Lowering his voice, he imitated his assistant's gravelly
tone. "'Go get some ice on that.' 'See the trainer for
some ice.'"

At sixteen, Dylan had been led to believe there
wasn't anything that couldn't be solved with enough ice
or some pacing.

Steve Asbury harrumphed, but his gray eyes twin-
kled with humor as he shook his head at his longtime
boss. "You know we're not going to miss you, old man."

"Liar," Coach Burton said confidently. "And good luck
replacing me. You ever think about it, Dylan? Coaching?"

Dylan coughed, stunned by the question. As far back
as first grade, he'd desperately wanted to get *out* of
school; he couldn't imagine voluntarily returning to
one.

"No, sir. Can't say that I have." Could he stand it,
watching young kids with the same dreams he'd once
harbored, doing what he was no longer able to? He
shuddered.

The coach eyed him. "The biggest requirements are
patience and a love of baseball. I used to ask a lot of you
guys in ninety-degree practices and during games. This
is the last thing I'll ask of you—think about it? For me."

Reluctantly Dylan nodded, trying to ignore the way
Barb was practically vibrating with excitement in her
seat. He'd resolved to come visit her more, but that did
not mean he wanted to move back to Mistletoe. He'd

promised Coach to at least consider it, though, so he would. Fleetingly.

His temples throbbed with the onset of a headache. So far on his weekend away from work, he'd become preoccupied with a woman who viewed the truth as nothing more than a loose guideline, he'd been swamped with guilt over what a bad son he was and now he found himself faced with unexpected career questions. Maybe next vacation, he'd try scaling Everest. It might be more relaxing.

Chapter Eight

Dressed in clothes Natalie had helped her pick out and armed with several books' worth of theory and tips on feng shui, Chloe felt totally prepared. Until Dylan opened the door. He was wearing a white T-shirt with a pair of dark jeans, a timeless look that she was sure had never worked quite this well on any other man. Ever.

"Hi." He spoke before she found her voice. "You're earlier than I expected. I guess traffic was light today."

It had been easier than she'd anticipated to find her way to his neighborhood. She'd even had a few minutes to grab something to drink at a trendy coffee shop around the corner and study some final crib notes. Learning new things—and learning them well—had always been something she enjoyed, and a certain part of her was eager to apply her newly acquired knowledge.

Dylan backed up to let her in, his warm gaze falling across her body like a sunbeam. "You look nice."

"Thank you." The bright pink, sleeveless V-neck

blouse was Natalie's, worn underneath a beige light-weight blazer of Chloe's. According to Nat, the matching beige skirt was saved from being boring by a pair of cute sandals and Chloe's "great legs."

"So this is 'professional C.J.,'" he said, an odd note in his voice. "You are a woman with many sides."

She smiled weakly and followed him into the living room. The couch sat with its back to the entryway, and his decorating choices were full of sharp edges.

"Bad chi," she mumbled.

"Pardon?" Dylan was studying her intently. Very intently. As if looking for something specific.

Or maybe, since she had something to hide, she was paranoid. She set her purse on a shiny black table and passed by Dylan to sit on the far end of the couch. "I should tell you, I'm…not the best decorator out there."

"I hope that isn't what you have printed on your business cards." He cocked his hip against the arm of the sofa, facing her but not exactly sitting with her.

"I just meant that lots of people probably work in this area and have more expertise. I'll tell you what I know, but you have to decide for yourself what speaks to you. It's *your* space," she said, wanting to absolve herself of as much responsibility as possible. "You ever see some of those redecorating shows on cable? Professionals charge a lot of money to do things to people's homes that occasionally make me cringe." She'd watched a few such shows this week and, while she'd thought jokingly of scaring Dylan off with feathers, one designer actually did incorporate feather trims and animal prints. Heavily.

"Decorating isn't like math," she continued. "There's

no set equation or one right answer. Even in feng shui, there are differences of opinion between traditionalists and modern practitioners. So don't take anything I tell you too seriously. It's just my opinion."

"But people pay you for that opinion."

She wouldn't let it get that far. "This is just a pre-liminary consultation," she reminded him. "You may well decide not to hire me. My feelings won't be hurt if you go a different direction. At all."

He arched a brow. "Well, I appreciate your being so honest and up-front about it."

She managed not to flinch at his word choice. Now that she'd given her disclaimer, she wanted to share with him what she'd discovered. "Feng shui creates the most harmonious living space possible, with emphasis on the chi, or energy."

Since Dylan Echols was a "man's man" from a small Georgia town where coffee came in only one standard size and flavor—none of this four-dollar "venti" madness—she'd half expected him to be put off by dis-cussion of crystals, natural life force and the spiritual importance of wind chimes and mirrors. In fact, she was counting on it. Once they'd established that this was not his cup of green tea, they could casually part ways, her dignity and his both intact.

But he listened avidly as she gave a brief overview of feng shui's history and how it went beyond color schemes and new throw pillows, even encompassing the property on which the home was built.

She caught herself rambling and took a deep breath. "I figured you'd be looking at me like I was crazy by now."

"Is that the reaction you usually get from people?"

"I never know what reaction to expect." Especially since she'd never discussed this with anyone until now. "A lot of this comes across as pretty New Agey."

Apparently she'd misjudged his open-mindedness, which made her feel better about him and worse about herself. After all, she knew what it was like to be branded by a stereotype, how it could be superficially accurate without telling the whole story.

He spread his hands in a nonchalant gesture, a horizontal shrug. "You obviously don't know how superstitious athletes can be. I guarantee I've heard far more off-the-wall notions than anything you're going to say."

"'Superstitious' like lucky socks, or pagan idols in the locker rooms?" she kidded.

"A little bit of both. One guy I knew was dating a woman named Diane Denton when he got called up to The Show. Weeks after they broke up, he was with Amy Ash when he hit his first major league homer. Apparently his high school girlfriend fit the pattern, too. So it's a rule with him now."

"You're not telling me he only gets involved with women whose first and last name start with the same letter? You're putting me on," Chloe accused, unable to imagine a rational adult acting that way.

"He proposed to Leigh Ledbetter on their second date because it's tough to find women that meet the criteria and he had a major contract negotiation on the line."

"Did she accept?" Chloe asked incredulously.

"No." Dylan grinned. "She advised him to look into extensive counseling."

Chloe began to see his point. Rearranging furniture for a more harmonious living environment sounded far more logical than proposing to a near stranger because of her initials. "What about you? Any superstitions?"

All the humor left his face, and she regretted the impulsive question.

"If I *had* been the superstitious type," he said, "it wouldn't matter now, would it?"

"So on-air personalities don't have their own quirky habits?" she coaxed.

"You drove all this way for a consultation, and I got you off topic. Tell me more about how feng shui works," he said firmly.

She sighed, then crossed her legs and sat straighter, hoping to project authority. "There's a *ba gua,* energy map, for your house as a whole and within each individual room. The terminology varies depending on the source, but essentially the areas are travel, health and family, reputation, career, knowledge, children and creativity, wealth and love."

"So you can help me improve any of those areas?" he drawled, the gleam in his eyes suggesting that buying tablecloths was not what he had in mind.

"First and foremost," she said briskly, "is intention. If you want to improve or change something, rather than stressing over specific feng shui rules, picture what you want." Good advice for him, not her. She needed to *stop* picturing what she wanted, which was him kissing her again.

Dylan nodded. "Positive visualization. Coach Burton

was a big believer in that, too. I have to admit, it worked pretty well for me. Up to a point," he added softly.

Chloe was glad she was seated too far away to touch him. Every time she saw how much it hurt him not to be playing ball anymore, she wanted to comfort him. She wanted to stroke his shoulder, hold him, kiss him until he forgot his disappointment.

Think platonic thoughts. No stroking the would-be client! Since he'd introduced the coach in conversation, she asked, "How'd the banquet go?"

"It was…surprising."

When he didn't elaborate, she teased, "Don't tell me, a woman jumped out of a cake?"

"Since my mother ended up being my date, I'm happy to say, no, that was not the case. Actually, the coach made some suggestions about what I might do career-wise now that I'm not pitching."

She tilted her head. "You don't plan to stay with sportscasting?"

"It's a good job." He fidgeted, averting his eyes. "I'm lucky they wanted me."

There it was again, that latent insecurity that had tugged at her heart in her kitchen when he'd called himself "just a jock." Didn't he know he had plenty to offer outside the baseball diamond? She inched closer before she could stop herself.

"Dylan." Her voice came out low, not much more than a whisper.

He jerked his head up, startled, but his gaze quickly heated. She could feel an answering warmth thrumming through her body. He, too, was clearly remembering the kisses they'd shared the other night. And he was just as clearly planning to do it again.

Her pulse leaped. "I…"

He'd slid down onto the couch cushions, leaning toward her. "Yes?"

I think you're amazing, fastball or not. I want to hear you say my actual name—Chloe—because you would make it sound so sexy. I can't remember ever wanting a man like this.

"N-nothing." She told herself to put more distance between them, but his eyes possessed an almost hypnotic pull. "No, there is something. It might be presumptuous of me to mention this, but I should let you know that I do not get romantically involved with customers."

He reached out, trailing a finger over her cheek. "I haven't hired you yet."

Dylan hadn't planned to kiss her.

While he had, admittedly, first asked her to decorate because he'd been grimly amused at the thought of watching her hoist herself on her own petard, he would never toy with a woman sexually. But the attraction to Chloe was as potent now as it had been when he'd first glimpsed her sitting in the Mistletoe Inn.

More so in spite of her confusing behavior and his infuriated humiliation when he'd learned she'd lied to him. To his surprise, he genuinely liked talking to her, loved the slow break of her smile. He knew details about her she didn't even realize, and he hungered for more.

Cupping her face, he bent forward and claimed the kiss he'd wanted ever since she'd bolted from his hotel room. He traced the seam of her lips with his tongue, pulled back just enough to grin down at her. "Tart."

Her eyes were wide amber pools. "*You* kissed *me,*" she protested.

He frowned, then threw his head back and laughed as her meaning set in. "Your lip gloss is tart."

"Oh. Pink lemonade," she informed him.

"It's different."

"Different, bad?"

When she would have wiggled away, he gently tightened his hold. "Not sure. I'm still forming an opinion." He lowered his mouth to hers.

She kissed him back thoroughly. Trustingly. It would be so easy to keep going, to lay her down on the couch and explore her delectable body. At the back of his mind was the dim echo of Nick's words, that Chloe didn't know how lovely she was. *I could show her.* Dylan could make her feel every inch a sexy goddess, deserving of lavish adoration.

At least, he could if she ever told him the truth about herself. She owed him that. Now that his initial anger had abated and he was enjoying her company so much, he was starting to genuinely care for her. Did she care enough about him to admit what she'd done? Regretfully he let his hands slide from her shoulders.

"Does this mean you've formed your opinion?" she asked, her voice low and entirely too tempting.

"Yes. In my opinion, you're addictive." He stood, not trusting himself to look at her because he'd probably reach for her again. "I should probably give you a tour of the rest of the place."

"Okay." She rose, too, and he hid a grin when he noticed she seemed a bit wobbly on her feet. Whatever else he might be confused about, he loved the idea that his kisses weakened her knees.

Dylan lived in a four-story building that had been erected in the late 1920s and had been revamped in recent years to make each story its own condo. An elevator from the parking garage led to interior entrances, but there were also back doors to the individual apartments, available by outside stairs. He had the top floor. The view wasn't that exciting since his windows just looked out at the sides of taller buildings, but he liked not having to worry about upstairs neighbors tromping around overhead.

His apartment was a big space, bisected by a slim foyer. On one side was a huge master bedroom. The kitchen, full bath and living room took up the other half. He led her to the kitchen first, and watched her scrutinize the stainless-steel appliances and gleaming white cabinets and counter.

"I have to hand it to you—you don't suffer from clutter. But don't you find it a bit…sterile?" she ventured. "A plant in here would do wonders, even if it was artificial. You know Nat runs the flower shop in town? I'll bet she could make some great suggestions. Or a few color accents would help. In feng shui, all colors have meanings, usually tied to the five Chinese elements—earth, fire—"

"Wind?"

She frowned at the interruption, looking adorably like a librarian shushing a rowdy patron. All that was missing from the picture were a pair of wire-rim glasses perched on her nose and maybe a pencil behind her ear.

"No," she corrected. "Earth, fire, metal, wood and water. Also known as the five transformations."

What the hell had she done? Memorized a feng shui textbook? Four days ago, he would have sworn she didn't know the first thing about the topic. Irritation flared. She was supposed to be backing down, floundering over her head and confessing her ruse. Once she apologized, he could magnanimously forgive her. Instead, she'd thrown herself wholeheartedly into the charade.

Waxing philosophical about colors, she didn't realize she'd temporarily lost her audience. "And then there's red, which is often thought to be the most powerful—"

"I'll say." Even annoyed he couldn't help admitting, "Seeing you in the hotel lobby, in that red dress, stopped me in my tracks. The fact that we were both there for the reunion was sheer luck. I would have been compelled to come talk to you even if I'd never seen you before in my life."

She swallowed, her throat rippling with the motion. His eyes trailed downward. Had he ever found a woman's collarbone sexy before Chloe? He didn't let himself dwell on any of the tantalizing places lower. He wanted this woman. But not until she owned up to what she'd done. Growing up with a learning disability, with Michael Echols for a father, Dylan had been made to feel like a fool far too many times. Chloe had deliberately deceived him, made him feel stupid, and there had to be *some* kind of consequence for that.

"No one's ever been moved to cross a room just to get to me," she said.

He would have pegged her words as more guile than truth if not for that jackass Petey Grubner's comments. Klutzy Chloe? A book nerd who never left her computer monitor? Was the male population of Mistletoe freaking blind?

"Men have noticed you," he told her, thinking of his friend Nick. "Maybe you just weren't sending the right signals to encourage their approach."

"Signals?" She cast him a dubious smirk. "You mean like tight tank tops or asking a guy what his sign is?"

"Please. Has anyone actually used a line like that since the seventies?" Although he wouldn't necessarily complain if she wanted to wear a skimpy top. "I meant body language. It's not that different from feng shui. You have to decide what your intentions are, what you're open to, and put that energy out there."

Instead of mocking what had sounded far lamer out loud than it had in his head, she nibbled at her lower lip, pondering his advice. Funny. He'd never been the type of person people came to for personal guidance. Jokes, yes. Pitching tips, maybe. Anything resembling wisdom, no.

"Your body language right now?" He met her eyes. "Very inviting."

"How so?"

"An open stance, angled ever so slightly toward me. Parted lips. Frequent eye contact, dilated pupils."

"Could just be the lighting," she quipped.

His mouth quirked in a half grin. "Could be." He

lowered his gaze briefly to the rise and fall of her chest. "A change in your breathing."

"Could be a respiratory condition."

He shook his head at her even as he chuckled. "And you wonder why some guys might not have the courage to pursue you?"

"Point taken. But didn't we establish that, as a client, you—"

"*Potential* client. You know, just to keep the boundaries clear, we should settle that once and for all." He reached for a kitchen drawer, pulling out the checkbook he kept there. Time to take this up a notch. "How much is your retainer fee or whatever decorator's call the initial deposit?"

Alarm flared in her eyes. "Oh, it's too soon for that. What if you hate my ideas? You—"

"I insist. Like you said, my space, my decision. So what's the name of your company? Or do I just make this out to Candy Beemis?" he challenged.

"C. W. Designs." Since she said it without a trace of hesitation, he figured it really was the name of her self-owned business.

"Not C.J. or C.B.?" he pushed. *Or C.M., Ms. Malcolm?*

"It's C.W.," she repeated, seeming unaware of the faint sarcasm in his voice.

"So what's the *W* stand for?"

She looked past him, her gaze unfocused as she smiled. "Wheezy. I actually did have a respiratory condition. I was born premature and had several lung problems and childhood asthma. So my aunt called me Wheezy."

"That's horrible!" Right up there with an adult calling a dyslexic kid an idiot. His free hand fisted involuntarily.

"No, you don't get it. It wasn't insulting." Chloe shook her head adamantly. "It was more… I don't know. I hated having asthma. I felt different from the other kids. Limited. And I *dreaded* being teased about anything. By turning it into a term of endearment, Aunt Jane took the sting out of it. It was liberating."

"Oh." He relaxed his fingers against his side, realizing he must have looked foolish, wanting to ride to her rescue years after the fact and pummel anyone who'd wounded her feelings. He half wished Petey Grubner was handy just so he could slug him. "That sounds like a healthy attitude."

"Yeah, maybe." She took a sudden keen interest in her manicure. "Not all of my coping strategies have been quite that well-adjusted, I'm afraid."

"Such as?" He lowered the pen and stared at her, trying to radiate empathy and understanding. *Tell me. You can tell me.*

He was angry that she'd lied to him last weekend, but he was beginning to see a bigger picture. Her favorite aunt had just died, and Chloe was acting out; she'd been at a reunion with people who'd apparently mocked her throughout high school while he'd been too busy with baseball—okay, and redheads—to notice the social angst of people around him. It was an unscrupulous thing she'd done, pretending to be Candy, and he'd never had any tolerance for cheaters.

Yet the more he learned about Chloe Malcolm, the

more he unwillingly sympathized. How had she felt when he'd mistaken her for Candy? Had he somehow cemented Chloe's fear that people saw her first and foremost as a nerd and not as the lovely woman she'd become?

Shifting her weight, she nodded toward the check-book. "I'm here on your dime. We're supposed to be talking about what you want to do with your place, and I'm treating it like a free therapy session. Why don't you show me the other rooms."

He gestured toward the microscopic hallway. "Not much else to show. The bathroom and bedroom are both right through there. With me, it's 'what you see is what you get,' C.J."

Since she was already moving ahead of him, he couldn't tell if she had any reaction to his comment.

His bathroom was modestly sized but equipped with all the basics. Chloe poked her head in, muttered to herself for a moment, then withdrew. Next, they walked into his room. He flipped on the light, and her gaze went immediately to the king-size bed. He could have sworn he saw a slight tinge of pink color her cheeks.

She glanced upward, pointing at the ceiling. "You have an exposed beam over where you sleep."

It ran the length of the room. "What does that mean?" he wanted to know.

"Sha chi, bad energy. Could be problematic."

"You sure? I've never had problems in the bedroom," he said, completely straight-faced.

Her blush deepened. "Still. There are things you can place to offset sha chi. Mirrors, for instance, are sup-posed to be pretty powerful."

He grinned. "You want me to put a mirror on my bedroom ceiling?"

"No! I mean, you could if you— No, that's not what I was suggesting. You could also affix a, um, bird figurine to the beam."

He followed her gaze skeptically. "A bird?" Frankly, the mirror idea had sounded more intriguing. "Not really me."

"Or a string of miniature lights," she babbled. "Bamboo flutes. You know what? Now that I've seen the place, I should take some time to think everything over. Write up some suggestions for you. I'll e-mail you!"

"Or we can get together next time I'm in Mistletoe," he said, mentally running through his work schedule. He had next Tuesday off and could stay at his mom's before heading back to Atlanta on Wednesday. While he'd tackled a couple of maintenance issues around his mom's house, there was more that needed to be done. "I'll be back in town next week."

"But you never come home!"

He arched an eyebrow. "You pay attention? I'm moved."

"Everyone does," she backpedaled. "You're a big deal in Mistletoe."

"Was. I *was* a big deal. Now I'm just—"

"Please don't do that." She touched his arm. "You're not 'just' anything. You're Dylan Echols. You're…" She trailed off, but the expression in her eyes made him very glad to be himself, to be on the receiving end of a look like that from a woman like her.

He knew better than to kiss her again, but he

couldn't help running his thumb across her bottom lip. "Thank you."

   If only she'd been so clear about who *she* was.

Chapter Nine

Chloe waited until she was clear of the Atlanta freeways before reaching for her cell phone at a red light. She punched in the first number programmed in her speed dial. "I'm a terrible human being! You shouldn't even be friends with me."

Her unorthodox greeting was met with a slight pause. "Chloe, is that you? I know a lot of terrible human beings, so you'll have to be more specific."

"This is serious, Nat. I'm out of control! You won't believe what happened at Dylan's place."

Natalie gasped. "Don't tell me you had sex with him. On second thought, do tell me. I want all the details."

"What? No, of course I didn't sleep with him! Although I was in his bedroom. And we did kiss again."

He was *such* a great kisser. He was a great listener. He was a great guy…which made her feel like slime. Today was supposed to have been the end of it. She was supposed to have freaked him out with girlie suggestions of angel figurines and crystal balls in every room, putting to rest the possibility of his wanting to hire her. But everything had gone wrong.

Paradoxically it had felt right.

He had a way of looking at her that made her feel sexy and whole and...*herself*. Even though she was pretending to be someone else, he seemed to see more of the real Chloe than her Web site customers, parents and friends. More than anyone except Natalie. In fact, Chloe thought, recalling the way they'd joked with each other, spending time with him was a lot like being with Natalie. Except that Nat knew Chloe's actual name and profession, and Chloe never fantasized about kissing her friend.

"Who kissed who?" Natalie asked, sounding ecstatic instead of outraged.

"It was sort of a mutual thing." Which she'd instigated, scooting closer to him on the couch. She didn't even want to think about how she must have been looking at him to encourage him. "That's not the point, anyway. I took his money!"

"You stole from him?"

"I might as well have! I let him write me a check for services rendered. Or to be rendered." She'd thrown out the lowest number that was still halfway credible, adding at his disbelieving expression that he got a discount because he was someone she knew. *But you live in a very small town,* he'd argued. *Don't you know about sixty percent of your clients? How do you stay in business if you give everyone that rate?*

It was difficult to lie to an astute man. Witness how he'd described seeing her at the inn, how he'd described her body language this afternoon—

"Hello? Did I lose you?" Natalie prompted. "Are you going through a bad reception area?"

"I'm going through a midlife crisis! And I'm not even thirty. I should have been racked with remorse all afternoon, but you know what the most shameful part is? I *enjoyed* myself." Especially the kissing. "I'm sick and twisted enough that most of me is *glad* he's coming to Mistletoe next week."

Even though she knew that every time he stepped foot inside town limits, it increased the odds that he'd find out she wasn't Candy Beemis and that C.J. the Decorator didn't even exist, her idiot heart beat a bit faster at the thought of seeing him again.

"Coming to Mistletoe?" Natalie shrieked. "To see you? This is incredible."

"I'm sure his main reason for the trip is to check on his mom, but he does want to see me while he's there. I gave him my cell number." She thought it was safer for him to have that, rather than the home number under Malcolm. It disturbed her that she'd even thought to take that precaution.

This was bad. The more she covered her butt, the deeper the hole she dug. At first, she'd told herself that he would be gone from her life soon, none the wiser. And now… Chloe had waited twenty-seven years to feel this way, alive and important, to have someone show avid interest in her as a woman, not as a sickly child too frail to be left unattended for a few minutes. Though it was insanity to continue on this course, the thought of pushing Dylan away for good pierced her like a wound. *Not yet, just a little more time. A few more memories.*

"So how'd you leave things with him?" Natalie wanted to know.

"I told him I'd work on design ideas for his place and that he could call me Monday or Tuesday. Nat, what am I *doing?*"

"I have no idea."

Chloe sighed, raising her gaze skyward and checking the clear blue horizon for celestial assistance. She was certain that if she had a guardian angel, it was Aunt Jane. There was also no doubt she was the only angel up there with a naughty enough streak to help out under these circumstances. "I really like him."

"Sure seems as if he likes you, too."

"Yeah, but there's no future in that. What am I supposed to do, date him, get him to fall in love with me, hope for every girl's dream proposal, then pray he doesn't notice the name on the marriage license? The only other option is to somehow explain to him that I've been lying. No way he'd want anything to do with me after that, and I wouldn't blame him. Who wants to be involved with someone they can't trust?" She tightened her grip on the steering wheel, cradling the phone between her ear and shoulder. "Do you think I could convince him that I sustained a major head injury shortly before the reunion? Forget I asked that."

When she figured out a way to be honest with Dylan, the key would be actual *honesty*. In the meantime, she was not cashing the check she'd guiltily stowed in her glove compartment. She also had no plan to kiss him when she saw him next week.

No matter how badly she was tempted.

MOST MEN WERE probably motivated by anniversaries and apologies to stop at flower stores. Dylan, pulling into town midmorning on Tuesday, was passing Mistletoe Berries and Blooms when he was suddenly inspired to go on a fishing expedition. Parking his car, he wondered what exactly he thought he might learn. Natalie and Chloe were obviously close—albeit not through the cheerleading bond he'd first assumed—but even though the blonde probably knew all sorts of details about her friend, she was unlikely to share them.

A small copper bell tinkled overhead, announcing his entrance to the shop.

"Hello?" a female voice called out from a small room behind the counter. Natalie came into view seconds later.

"Hi, there." He smiled, pouring on as much charm as was possible without hitting on her or trying to sell her a car.

"Dylan. I have to say, I'm surprised to see you here."

Surprised, but not shocked, which would have been a legitimate reaction since he hadn't set foot in the flower shop since he'd picked up his date's corsage for the senior prom. Had Chloe told her friend he was coming to town? The idea of Chloe talking about him left him feeling divided. On the one hand, it was nice thinking that she might care enough about him to confide in someone else. But if Chloe *had* been discussing him, would she also have told Natalie about her impersonation? That possibility rankled.

"I was hoping you'd be in today." He kept his tone easy. "Maybe you can help me pick out an arrangement for C.J.? I don't want it to be too intimidating or clichéd—no dozen red roses—but since she arranges beautiful things for a living, I want it to be special."

"Sure thing." Natalie didn't even blink. Or ask, *C.J. who?*

Though he wasn't surprised she knew about the situation, his gut clenched anyway. It had been galling the night of the reunion to find out he'd been made a fool of—it was worse that someone else was aware. Had Chloe revealed her tall tale only to Natalie or were there other people in Mistletoe who knew? A sickening sensation enveloped him as he too easily imagined a conspiracy in which townfolk nodded to his face and laughed behind his back. In his head, he heard Grady Medlock's snickers, the titters of classmates when he'd been asked to read aloud during those early years before baseball had elevated his status to a popular student.

If you could throw an amazing curveball and owned a varsity letter jacket, your peers didn't care whether or not you were struggling with Shakespeare and Steinbeck. Not that the varsity jacket fit anymore.

"Dylan?" Natalie's blue eyes looked so genuinely concerned that it would be easy to hold it against her, knowing that behind her facade of friendly worry she was party to deceiving him. At least she was a smoother liar than Chloe, so it wasn't as much of an insult to the intelligence.

"Are you all right?" she asked.

"Just second-guessing myself," he heard himself say. "Maybe the flowers aren't such a good idea."

"No, wait. I think they're a wonderful idea."

"You're the flower purveyor," he pointed out. "Of course *you're* in favor of it."

"True. But—and she would kill me dead if she knew

I was saying this—she likes you." Natalie waited a beat, perhaps waiting for some assurance that the feeling was mutual. When she didn't get it, she tensed slightly. "I hope that your being back in Mistletoe so soon, thinking about flowers, means that she wasn't just someone to chat with at the reunion. I'd hate to see her hurt."

Whoa, back the hell up, Mama Bear. He understood protective loyalty among friends, but from his point of view, Natalie should be issuing warnings *about* Chloe to unsuspecting men, not issuing warnings on her behalf.

"I'll keep that in mind," he said tightly.

"I overstepped, didn't I? It's really none of my business what happens between the two of you."

The remorse in her tone made him sigh—she wasn't the one who'd started this mess. "You were looking out for someone you care about. I get it."

"Thank you. I do care about her. We're both only children, more like sisters than friends. God knows I might not have earned my diploma without her."

Dylan thought about how Nick had said more or less the same thing.

"And I'm probably more worried about her right now than I ordinarily would be. She just lost someone who meant a lot to her."

"Her aunt?" He nodded. "Jane sounds like quite the character."

"Oh, she was." Natalie smiled fondly, then her expression became more somber. "I'm sure you know what it's like to be turned emotionally upside down by losing someone. It wasn't too long ago that your father…" She trailed off, probably realizing she was overstepping again.

If he were a different sort of son—if Michael Echols had been a different sort of father—Dylan would buy flowers for the grave while he was here. It was the decent thing to do. He could just imagine how such an action would cheer his mom, who'd always liked to pretend there was nothing wrong in her home.

Gritting his teeth, Dylan thought about how much the pretense had bothered him, the hypocrisy of his old man cheering for him at games, acting the proud father when happily accepting accolades from everyone else in the bleachers while, at home, he made his son feel like nothing he ever did was good enough.

And now Dylan was knowingly turning his own personal life into a pretense? The truth was, he did like Chloe. But he wasn't sure he liked himself for it.

At TEN O'CLOCK, Chloe met with Kimberley Warren, a local matron with four kids. Kim was opening a salon in the back of her house and wanted to talk about the possible cost of a Web site. Knowing that Dylan was supposed to reach town today, Chloe found herself losing her concentration more than she had when she was a teenager sitting in class with him. Luckily, with children ranging from a tired-but-refusing-to-nap six-month-old to an eight-year-old home from school after getting tubes in her ears yesterday, Kim was too distracted herself to notice Chloe's momentary lapses.

Kim grimaced at the third consecutive interruption, a request for something to drink. "Can you give me just a second? The oldest one isn't usually this much of a pain. She's just bored silly because she's cooped up at home. Honestly, if I'd realized how easy her recovery was going to be, I would have sent her to class."

"I don't mind at all," Chloe said. Her next appointment, with Rachel Waide, wasn't for another two hours. Plus, ever since Rachel and her husband, David, had found out they were expecting, the woman was extra indulgent about anything involving children. She wouldn't mind if Chloe ran a few minutes late.

The beleaguered mommy poured some grape juice and exited the kitchen muttering. As Chloe waited, she found herself looking around and evaluating the room. Round table, which was good chi, but the stove was not optimally placed, in conflict with— Chloe blinked when she realized the direction her thoughts had taken. *You know you're not* actually *a decorator, right?*

Still, she'd found herself inspired over the weekend, brainstorming some ideas for her own home. It wasn't a bad little house and she certainly had some fond memories of growing up there, but she was an adult now. Wasn't it time to make it *her* place and not her parents'? She hadn't started any projects yet, but she'd put together an outline of what she wanted to accomplish and gone window-shopping Sunday afternoon to compare prices on supplies.

"Sorry about that." Kim came back into the room. "But I think that's the last of the interruptions. I told the eight-year-old we could order pizza for lunch if she can find something to watch in the DVD collection until then, and the baby finally fell asleep in his playpen."

"Not a problem. Now, about some simple things you could do for a site…"

They tossed around some ideas, including Kimberley's desire to include pictures of Mistletoe locals, which she could update periodically. As Chloe started getting more into the technical side of things, she realized Kim was staring at her absently.

"Did I lose you?" Chloe asked.

"What? Oh, it's not that. I was just wondering… Would you let me cut your hair? Then we could take a picture! You'd be one of the first photos for my online portfolio, and it would be my way of saying thanks for today. Well, more than today. I swear every time we've talked on the phone, one of the kids has been playing drums in the next room, tattling on a sibling or inciting the dog to bark in the background."

Chloe laughed. "It hasn't been too bad."

"Is that your polite way of turning down the haircut?"

Now that Chloe thought about it, when was the last time she'd had a trim? Her thoughts skittered back to Dylan. She'd be seeing him soon. It wouldn't hurt to look her best. "Okay, sure. We could take off a few split ends."

"You don't want anything else done?" Kim looked disappointed. "I was hoping for something at least dramatic enough for 'before' and 'after' pictures."

Chloe smoothed her hand over her head. Barring the short-lived and ill-advised highlights when she was a teen, she'd worn her hair pretty much the same way ever since…what, second grade? Good Lord. She was a one-woman definition of *stagnant*.

Not anymore. "What did you have in mind?"

Kim brightened. "I'm glad you asked!"

FAR FROM the somewhat timid woman Dylan often remembered her as, Barb Echols seemed positively jubilant now, flitting about her kitchen and humming while she prepared lunch for the two of them. She was so happy that Dylan found himself grinning, her mood contagious. For a little while, he forgot Chloe Malcolm and simply took pleasure in having made a right decision.

"I was so excited when you called to say you were coming back!" Instead of being discouraged that he couldn't stay longer, his mom was obviously touched. "Some people wouldn't even think the drive was worth it for only an overnight stay."

"It's not that far." The trip was not even two hours. He knew people in the Atlanta area who commuted close to that just to get to work. It was not a hardship for him to get in the convertible, turn up the MP3 player and drive on a sunny day.

Barb stirred a pot of her homemade chicken noodle soup, the peppery aroma that wafted from the pot immediately taking him back to childhood. "Still. With gasoline prices what they are these days… I'm so glad to see you. You know who else would be equally happy? Todd."

Dylan was so accustomed to everyone he knew calling Todd Burton "Coach" that it took him a second to make the connection. "Coach B.?"

His mother nodded. "Have you talked to him since the banquet? About his offer?"

Suddenly restless, Dylan stood. He busied himself

getting bowls down for the soup. Unfortunately that only killed about three seconds.

"It wasn't really an 'offer,' Mom, merely a suggestion. He can't just hand out a job. I'm sure there's a lot of bureaucracy with the school board involved."

Barb hesitated; he assumed she'd agree with him and change the subject. It's what she would have done in a similar situation if she'd been talking to his father. So Dylan was startled to see her square her shoulders, lift her chin and shake her silvered head at him.

"That's silly, and you know it. With your record in the sport and Coach Burton's sway in this community, you could probably walk into the school's administration office this afternoon and have the position before dinner." As if realizing how vocal she was being with her opinion, she lowered her gaze, mumbling, "If you wanted it."

Passing behind her on the way back to the table, he stopped to give her a quick squeeze of affection. *Go, Mom.* He didn't want the job, but he was thrilled to see his mother showing some spirit. "I'm not convinced that I'd be a good coach. Besides, some people in Atlanta pulled strings to help get me into a really good job after my shoulder gave out. It seems wrong to just walk away from that."

"So you'll stay in a situation you know deep down isn't right for you because you feel obligated?" Her voice cracked.

"Mom." Instead of taking his seat, he returned to her. "You okay?"

"No. I'm an old woman looking back on her life."

He hugged her to his chest. "You're not old."

"I feel it," she muttered into his shirt. "I've felt old for *years*. And now I…now I…"

Oh, damn. She was crying, and Dylan didn't have the first clue what to do. Irrationally he wished Chloe were here. Next to his mother, Chloe was currently the central female in his life, and this seemed like an occasion requiring a feminine touch. She'd been sensitive and insightful at his apartment. So what would Chloe do in this situation? *Probably lie through her teeth.* Not helpful.

"I'm getting your shirt all wet," Barb sobbed.

"I have plenty of shirts, but only one mother." He led her to the table and she sat down. "I want to help."

"Such a good boy. And after you were handed such a poor lot in life."

He squirmed guiltily—he'd endured his difficult adolescent years surrounded by friends and admiring peers, had gone on to follow his dream and had been able to pursue it further than most men ever did. "It's not so bad. I played major league ball for a few seasons. Even now I have decent gig. I also have people here who love me, like you and Coach."

"I know it was hard on you," she insisted. "The struggles at school. Before you found baseball, I was always scared to death you'd drop out before you graduated. I wanted more for you than I ever accomplished. I got married so young I never even *considered* college. And you have a diploma and a degree!"

She wasn't this upset about his dyslexia, and they both knew it. It wasn't just school that had been an ordeal. The fact of the matter was, sometimes being there had been a nice respite from being home.

He shoved a hand through his hair. "I don't want to talk about him."

"I don't blame you. Looking at the man you've become, I wonder if I did the right thing staying here all these years or if I should have… I don't know what I would have done without your father, but maybe it was only cowardice that kept me from finding out, not love." Her eyes filled again. "Is it wrong to look at this as a fresh start? There was a time I loved him, there must have been."

She looked unconvinced, but Dylan was the wrong man to plead his father's case.

Dashing away a few tears, she added in a stronger tone, "I do want you to know he loved you. In his own way, he loved you very much. I don't know if he ever told you this, but his mother had a learning disability. Not that it was diagnosed well or that school curricula back then were developed to handle that. I think your father had a misplaced sense of anger, that maybe you'd inherited something through him."

"Mom, I know you have the best of intentions, but I do not want to talk about it." To lessen the sting of his vehement words, he knelt by her chair. "We *should* look at this as a fresh start, with each other. Please don't beat yourself up over what-ifs. You can second-guess your plays all you want, but it still won't change the score after the game's finished. The truth is, I wasn't an ideal son, either. But we can work on that, right?"

"Right." She gave him a watery smile, emboldened.

"And we could work on it even more if you took a coaching job in Mistletoe."

AFTER LUNCH, Dylan attempted to distract himself from everything his mom had said by calling Chloe to let her know he'd reached town, but her cell phone rolled immediately to voice mail. *You've reached C. W. Designs,* she chirped. *Leave a message, and I'll call you back as soon as I can!* The cynical part of him wondered if that had always been her outgoing recording, or if she'd altered it and removed her name since giving him her number. Having struck out getting in touch with her, he tried Nick Zeth instead.

Nick laughed as soon as Dylan identified himself. "Dude, when I offered to buy you dinner next time you were in town, it's because I figured you wouldn't be back for at least a decade. What happened, you get back to Atlanta and decide you missed us?"

The picture of Chloe's smile swam in his memory. "Something like that. But don't worry, I'm not looking for a free meal. Maybe just some company at batting practice?" He had sworn to his mentor to at least consider the idea of coaching. Now, with Barb adding her own pressure, Dylan felt that, at a minimum, he should swing by the high school to watch the team for a few minutes this afternoon.

Showing up might make him look more interested in the job than he really was, though. He planned to use Nick as a human shield, just two former players motivated by recent nostalgia to check out the old stomping grounds and see the new team in action.

"I can get away for a little while," Nick agreed. "I'm not active today, just on call. I'll bring the pager with me."

Once they were off the phone, Dylan called the school to verify that practice time hadn't changed and to make sure Coach Asbury didn't mind the audience.

"Hell, no. You boys feel free to come down on the field and give pointers. I don't suppose you'd be willing to autograph baseballs for the kids?"

Dylan winced. "Maybe next time. I think we'll keep it low-key and incognito today."

He arrived in the bleachers wearing shades and a scruffy cap pulled down over his forehead.

Nick smirked at him. "No one told me we were wearing spy gear. I would have brought my trench coat and fake mustache."

"I wanted to observe without being blatant about it," Dylan admitted. The boys down on the field had just begun their warm-up exercises.

"Does this have anything to do with Coach B. informing anyone who will listen that you're his natural successor?"

"Tell me he's not," Dylan implored.

"Only if you don't mind me lying to your face."

"No thanks, I've had quite enough of that lately," he grumbled. Witnessing Nick's transparent curiosity, Dylan engaged in a brief mental debate and decided he might as well get someone else's take on the situation. After all, Chloe had a confidant. *Turnabout is fair play.* "You remember my asking about Chloe Malcolm?"

"Yeah, she caught your eye at the reunion."

"More than caught my eye. We talked for a while. I may have even kissed her."

"You're not *sure?*" Nick drawled.

"I was trying to give you the pertinent information but still be a gentleman about it."

"Sorry, just having fun. Continue."

"During the course of our conversation, she lied to me about who she was. I had to resort to skimming through reunion literature just to figure out who the hell I'd had up in my hotel room!"

"Hotel room?" Nick gave a fierce shake of his head. "You can't be talking about Chloe Malcolm. None of this sounds like her."

"She called herself C.J. and told me she was an interior decorator. Unless she has an identical twin you forgot to mention?"

"No, she's an only child."

"Yeah, that's what her friend Natalie said, too." Dylan glared out at the baseball diamond, but barely processed what he was watching. "They're both in on it."

"'In on it'?" Nick echoed. "Chloe and Natalie Young? You make it sound like they deliberately set you up."

No. In retrospect Dylan caught the small hesitations that he'd overlooked the night of the reunion. "I don't think it was premeditated. I'm the one who mistook Chloe for Candy Beemis. She went along with it and then some, embellishing along the way." When he thought of her standing in the kitchen listing the five elements of feng shui as if she were the expert she claimed to be, he wanted to shake her.

Or at least kiss her senseless.

"You thought she was Candy Beemis?" Nick's jaw dropped. "How the hell could you confuse a sweet kid—Chloe—for that she-wolf?"

Sweet kid? "She's the same age we are," Dylan pointed out. "And not to disillusion you, but—"

"Did you actually call her Candy?" Nick clarified. "That had to sting. I know I temporarily lost my wits and dated Candy—I mean, come on, have you *seen* her? I was young and at the mercy of my hormones—but the girl has a vicious streak. Chloe always brought out the worst in her. It's not the reason she gave publicly, but I think Candy dumped me because I had the gall to suggest she lay off the jokes at Chloe's expense."

So Dylan had come along at the high school reunion, where Chloe might have been feeling vulnerable over the way people had treated her in the past, and immediately mistaken her for someone who'd made her teen years a living hell? Awkward. *But she should have just corrected me like a normal person!* His blunder didn't excuse her inventing a persona and perpetrating an elaborate hoax.

"What on earth did Chloe say when you asked her about all this?" Nick demanded.

Dylan's mouth twisted. "It's more complicated than that. When I asked if she went by Candy or Candace, she told me it was C.J. now and she led me to believe she was an interior decorator. So...I hired her."

"I've never heard that she does any decorating on the side," Nick argued, looking confused. "She works with computers."

"I know! But she doesn't know that I know."

"Dude, you're making my head hurt."

Welcome to my world. "Maybe she's bipolar. Maybe she's using me to live out some kind of fantasy." Although it wasn't the kind of fantasy he would have hoped. "All I can tell you is that she's gone to great lengths to pull one over on me. I don't want to just tell her the jig is up. I want her to admit what she's done and apologize." Soon, he fervently hoped.

Because he couldn't stop thinking about her. *She* had to be the one to set things right, but once she did, maybe they could see each other for real. Have that dinner they'd missed the night of the reunion, exchange more of those kisses that might lead—

"Wouldn't it just be easier to confront her? Or to walk away entirely? You can't actually let her decorate your place."

Then this probably wasn't the time to mention that Dylan was supposed to see her later to discuss swatches and furniture. "She took the check of her own free will," he defended himself, "passing herself off as a licensed decorator."

Despite Nick's logical suggestion, Dylan didn't think he *could* simply walk away. Though she had only re-entered his life a week and a half ago, Chloe had made quite an impact. The lust he'd felt when he first saw her, the anger when he'd learned who she really was—or wasn't—the compassion he'd felt when she talked about her aunt and the admiration when she mentioned her asthma, trying to pretend casually that didn't bother her anymore. He knew how tough it was to be a kid when you felt different from everyone else around you. Just about everyone Dylan knew had expressed some sort of condolence that he'd lost his ball career, but Chloe was different, the way she'd reached out to him at his condo. She'd made comforting him seem hot rather than pitying. The former was extremely preferable.

"I just can't wrap my mind around this," Nick said. "Chloe and Natalie lying and scheming? It's like finding out Bambi and Thumper are beating up the other forest animals for their lunch money."

"Life's not an animated fairy tale." Dylan's storybook ending would have involved a long career and a Cy Young Award. And what about his mother, married to an emotional bully and struggling with the regret thirty years later? Dylan was smart enough to accept reality rather than butt his head against it.

So why, whenever he thought of Chloe and the sweetness of her kiss, did he allow himself to imagine a happily-ever-after?

Chapter Ten

"I tumbled into the photography thing," Rachel bubbled, looking adorably round and almost too big for the precarious folding chair in the back room of the print shop. "I can't remember—pregnant-woman brain— what do you call happy accidents?"

"Serendipity?" Chloe offered.

Rachel snapped her fingers. "That's it! Pictures were a hobby, but then when the chamber of commerce approached me about doing a series for them, other opportunities presented themselves. It's been a slow trickle. Nothing close to what you'd call a full-time job, but that's not what I want after the baby comes, anyway. Just a supplemental income with flexible hours after I abandon poor May. But even for that, I think a Web site is a must."

Ever since Rachel got married and moved to Mistletoe, she'd worked for May Gideon, who was helping customers out front while Rachel used a late lunch hour to meet with Chloe. May had expressed regret that her friend was quitting in her final trimester, but couldn't be happier that it was to become a full-time mom.

"I can definitely help build you a site tailored to your needs," Chloe promised. "We just need to talk ab— Are you okay?"

"Fine. Sorry, didn't mean to scare you." Rachel's hands had jerked to her stomach so quickly Chloe had feared something might be wrong. "We'd been expecting to feel the baby move—'flutters,' all the books say—but nothing happened for the longest time. Dr. McDermott did an extra sonogram just to check on everything. Then this week, he—or she—started kicking up a storm. It's amazing."

"He or she? It's still too soon to determine the sex?" With the baby due this summer, Chloe would have thought they knew whether they were having a boy or girl by now.

"David and I decided to wait and find out." The woman's face lit up when she mentioned her husband. "We asked Dr. McDermott not to tell us, even though she knows. Maybe it's a little impractical, since it limits what we can buy ahead of time and I have to keep addressing it as The Baby, but—"

"I think it's cool that you'd rather not know," Chloe told her. "After all, when you stop and think about it, how many surprises are there really in life? This is a way to enjoy a huge one. Like throwing yourself a fantastic surprise party."

Rachel nodded happily, but with a faraway look on her face, her focus was clearly on her baby.

Chloe had never had a surprise party, but she would have hated it. In her life experience, "surprises" usually consisted of a sudden inability to breathe or a moment of social ineptness she immediately wanted to take back or the rare computer crash.

She preferred structure, logic, predictability.

Was that why she'd resisted the idea of the reunion so strongly—because she couldn't calculate what would happen, whether she'd be the newly created femme fatale Natalie hoped for or just Klutzy Chloe version 2.0? Unlike the aunt who'd lived each day as an unexpected adventure, on the eager brink of new discoveries and adventures, Chloe would probably spend the rest of her life here in Mistletoe. She'd gone into exactly the kind of field her instructors would have forecast for an introverted student good with computers. Her life didn't lend itself to surprise.

Until Dylan. The night of the reunion, Chloe had thought of herself rather sardonically as Cinderella. Now, however, she felt more like Sleeping Beauty. Had she been sleepwalking through her carefully ordered existence all these years? Suddenly the idea of waking up each day and wondering what could happen didn't seem like a terrible fate. It seemed…exciting.

"I can't believe how different you look," Rachel said, diverting her attention from the neonatal gymnastics back to Chloe.

"You mean my hair?" Chloe smiled shyly. Kim had layered it that morning, not taking off so much that it was tons shorter, but styling it so that the overall effect was quite different.

"Not just the hair. Everything! Your makeup, your clothes."

Was the change really so noticeable? Chloe was

wearing light powder, as usual, with mascara and gloss. It must be her blackberry gloss, which was darker and more dramatic than what she normally wore to a casual day meeting. The blue dress she'd chosen had been one of Aunt Jane's more conservative gifts, which still made it more daring than anything Chloe had bought for herself. She'd looked in the mirror that morning and grinned, pleased by what she saw. Pleased by the possibilities.

Leaning closer, Rachel added in a confidential tone, "And then there's the glow. Looking at you, I see what people must mean when they tell me I'm glowing."

Chloe blinked. "Well, I'm not pregnant. I can guarantee you that."

"No, that's not what I was implying." Rachel laughed. "You look like a woman in love."

"What?"

"So who is he? If it's anyone in town, I know him, right?"

"He's not in town exactly. And it isn't love. Maybe a crush." What was she, thirteen? *Dear Diary...* Chloe groaned, then murmured, "This is why I need C.J."

"His name's C.J.?"

"No. C.J. is a long story. Kind of a role model." Or, more accurately, alter ego. "She wouldn't fall apart at the mere mention of a man."

"If you makes you feel any better, I've fallen apart over David plenty of times," Rachel commiserated.

"I find that hard to believe." Chloe had seen the couple together often over the past few months. They looked like a perfect fit. Not in the sickeningly Stepford kind of way, just that they seemed so natural, as if it were a universally accepted equation. Like the fundamental theorem of calculus.

And completely un*like me and Dylan Echols.*

"Rachel, did you ever worry that maybe you and David didn't belong together?"

Chloe was shocked when the other woman burst into nearly hysterical laughter.

"Oh, honey. You have no idea." Rachel wiped an eye. "Trust me, there were days that we both questioned it. There was even a time when I almost walked away. But we ultimately realized our relationship was worth working on."

"I don't think what I have qualifies as a relationship," Chloe admitted.

"I am dying to hear more," Rachel said, her tone apologetic, "but I have a tiny person doing chorus-line kicks over top my bladder. Give me a sec?"

"Sure." Alone in the room, Chloe pulled out her cell phone, unable to resist checking messages. Had Dylan called? The suspense was killing her.

As soon as she saw his name and number appear on the tiny digital readout, she could feel her blood racing faster in her veins. She hesitated before listening, drawing out the moment, the way she sometimes paused before eating the last bite of a really exquisite dessert, savoring it. Then she gave in to curiosity and punched the button.

"Hi, it's Dylan. I'm here in Mistletoe…and I hope I can see you tonight. Call me?" Beneath his crisp, confident tone, there was a single boyish note that made her grin. She reached for a pen and paper, then replayed the message to catch his number at the end.

She'd just finished writing the digits when Rachel returned. The other woman stopped in the doorway, doing a double take of Chloe's broad smile and flushed cheeks. "I have no idea if you have a relationship or not," the other woman said, "but you definitely have *something* going on!"

The question was, what?

DYLAN WAS DRIVING home after leaving the high school when the cell phone played his John Fogerty "Center-field" ring tone. "'Lo?"

"Hi." Hearing Chloe's voice created the strangest sensation throughout his body, as if it subtly relieved certain tension he was carrying with him but created tight bands of something different altogether. "It's me."

"C.J.?" he pressed.

"Yeah. I got your message. So you're in town?" It was the same husky tone he'd first heard the night of the reunion.

He could close his eyes and listen to her talk like that for hours. "I'm here. Are you available tonight?"

"Very. You could come over again and—"

"Actually, why not come to my mother's for dinner?" It was an impulsive invitation, thrown out in part because he didn't trust himself with Chloe unchaperoned.

"Y-your mother? That would be Barbara Echols?"

"Yep. You know her?" That would certainly bring the situation to a head.

"Just by name," Chloe said. "Are you sure she won't mind?"

Barb would be thrilled, and Dylan discovered that he

wanted the extra time with her before leaving tomorrow. "Tell you what, I'll double-check with her. The tentative plan is that you'll come over and I'll cook—"

"You cook? Your kitchen was spotless. It didn't look as if anyone ever ate there, much less cooked there."

Spotless could have been a compliment, but her tone, not to mention her expression when she'd seen it, made him think that she really meant *barren*. Was his kitchen so devoid of personality? "Well, I don't spend hours on end simmering sauces and whipping up new culinary creations, but yeah, I can cook. If that's inconvenient for Mom, we'll go to the Dixieland Diner."

His suggestion was met with a long silence.

"Check with your mom," she said finally, "and we'll play it by ear. But one of our homes really would be convenient so we can take a look at a computer after we eat. There are some decorating sites I wanted to show you."

He agreed to call her back with the final verdict, then disconnected as he pulled into the driveway. His mother met him on the front porch.

"Did you have a nice time at practice?" she asked.

"I don't know. It's a lot to think about." The boys on the field had played with enthusiasm, but even watching them for a short time, he'd thought of several things he'd have them try differently. Still, he wasn't sure he was the man for the job. Players needed someone wise and motivational, like Coach. "Not to change the subject, but how would you feel if I had a friend over to dinner?"

"When you're in town, this is your home! You can have people over whenever you like," she assured him. "Is this one of the guys from the banquet? Nick or Shane?"

"No, this is a female acquaintance who wasn't there."

His mother pursed her lips thoughtfully. "The one who turned you down before you got stuck taking me?" Her green eyes were twinkling, making it clear she'd been teasing him.

"I was honored to have your company, Mom, but yes, it is the same young lady."

"So are the two of you an item?"

"No, she's going to help me redecorate my condo." It was a safe, convenient explanation that might stave off further questioning. "Until the reunion, we hadn't spoken in ten years, and we didn't run in the same circles in high school. To tell you the truth, I don't know her that well. But maybe…"

"Maybe?" His mother nodded sharply. "I'll take maybe for now."

"Great. You let me know what time works for you, and I'll call her back to hammer out the details. Then I might need to make a quick run to the store. Any special requests on what you'd like me to cook?"

"You cook?"

He didn't know whether to be amused or affronted by getting the same incredulous response twice. "Is it really that hard to believe? I've been living on my own for some time now. Did you think I just ordered pizza and nuked frozen entrées?"

She shrugged. "Other men have gotten by on less. I'm glad you have some domestic skills."

"Oh, I'm all over the domestic skills. Sometimes I get really wild and crazy and even do my laundry," he deadpanned.

Chuckling, she poked him in the ribs. "Don't get smart with your mother, son."

He looped his arm around her diminutive shoulders. "I love you, Mom."

It was startling to realize that he'd misjudged a woman he'd known his entire life. For years, he'd pegged her as someone too soft-spoken to be capable of mischievous humor, too weak to acknowledge difficult truths. But he'd only viewed a single, simplistic side of her.

If there was one thing Dylan had learned in the past two weeks, it was that people were always more complex than they appeared at first glance.

Chapter Eleven

"Whoa." Dylan couldn't help the long, lingering once-over of the beautiful woman on the other side of the doorway. "You look amazing."

He couldn't put his finger on everything that was different. Her overall appearance wasn't blatantly seductive as it had been for the reunion, but there was something more sensual about her than when she'd shown up at his apartment.

"Thank you." She held up a square cardboard box.

"Pizza in case I burn the chicken?" he surmised.

"No, I brought dessert. Key lime pie from the diner."

"My favorite."

"I know. I mean…I heard that once. And I have a pretty strong memory." She sighed. "You're going to get a restraining order now, aren't you?"

"No." He brushed a piece of her hair behind her ear, just for an excuse to touch her. "It's— Did you get a haircut?"

She nodded, looking pleased. "I thought guys never noticed stuff like that."

"Is whoever told you *that* stereotype the same person spreading the story that guys can't cook? People can be multifaceted, you know." He was only just beginning to see how true that was…and beginning to wonder how it applied to him.

For the majority of his life, he'd thought of himself as a ballplayer, but just because his career had ended didn't mean his life had. His thoughts flickered back to the practice he'd witnessed today. Despite what Dylan had told his mother about feeling obligated to Channel Six and the people who'd helped him get the job, he couldn't help entertaining possibilities. Did he possess enough of the qualities that made Coach Burton so special?

He showed Chloe inside. After placing the pie on the kitchen counter, he led her to the living room, where he knew his mother sat in genteel impatience, not wanting to hover but dying to meet Chloe.

"C.J., this is my mom, Barbara Echols." His hand went to the small of Chloe's back as he introduced the two women currently most important in his life, women with whom he was developing unexpected relationships.

His mother rose to shake Chloe's hand. "Oh, call me Barb."

"And, Mom, this is C.J." He felt Chloe tense as she worried that he'd add Beemis. He couldn't do it. He wanted Chloe and his mother to get along, which could be compromised if protective Barb learned later about Chloe's lies. Dylan himself still experienced twinges of residual anger, but he knew that he could forgive her deception. If he simply called her by name, it would put an end to this entire fiction. But would it also end a relationship between them before it had even begun? Instead of finding the courage to tell him herself, Dylan would take the choice away from her. He needed to know that she trusted him enough—that she could be trusted—to tell him on her own.

"You have a beautiful home," Chloe said. She gravitated toward the fireplace. The mantel was graced by three framed pictures of Dylan. When he'd lived here, his parents' wedding picture had dominated the ledge. Barb had removed it.

She joined Chloe. "If you want to see pictures, I have entire scrapbooks!"

"Mom, I'm sure—"

His mother sent an impish look over her shoulder. "Don't you have something you're supposed to be cooking?"

"Fine." He returned her heckling tone. "But see if I ever bring a date home again."

Chloe's body jerked at the word *date*. In profile, he could see a light blush staining her cheeks. Several comments came to mind, but his mom's presence stopped him from saying anything that might make Chloe more self-conscious.

After he'd retreated to the kitchen, he heard his mom poking around in the hall closet, looking for albums, followed by the murmur of female voices and occasional laughter.

It was ten minutes later that Chloe drifted into the kitchen. The change in her wasn't just the hair. He could swear she carried herself differently, as if she was more comfortable in her own skin. She'd been at least a little skittish during all of their previous encounters; this was the first time he'd seen her at ease.

"Anything I can do to help?" she asked.

He had just topped the barbecue chicken breasts with slices of provolone cheese. The potatoes were done. "You can pull the salad out of the fridge, if you'd like. And the bottle of dressing. Mom makes it herself."

"She's sweet," Chloe said, sounding genuinely affectionate and not like someone sucking up to her date.

"She likes you. She doesn't open up so quickly to everyone."

"Neither do my parents." Chloe carried the salad bowl to the table. "They can be very…insular. They have good hearts, they just aren't effusive. Or welcoming in the traditional outgoing sense. Even Natalie, who's known them forever, still calls them Mr. and Mrs.— Oh, shoot. I stubbed my toe."

He shot her a look of pure skepticism, but she wasn't meeting his eyes at the moment. Chloe was not cut out for lying. She was too artless and straightforward. When was she going to realize that she couldn't keep this up and just come clean?

Put us both out of our misery, sweetheart.

She took a shaky breath. "So…your mom tells me you might be interviewing for a coaching job at the school?"

"I don't know, maybe. But if I did get a job at Mistletoe High, we could finally have that dinner out I keep offering." Seeing the anxiety creeping into her gaze, he pressed further. "Unless, of course, you wouldn't be interested in seeing me socially? You've shot me down more than once. A man could get a complex."

"I'm interested," she murmured.

"Really? Sometimes it seems that you want to get away from me. Like in the grocery store parking lot, when I had to talk you into lunch. Or when you fled the reunion."

"That had nothing to do with you! There were extenuating circumstances."

"Such as?"

Chloe bit her bottom lip—hard from the looks of it. He wanted to rub his finger over the spot, soothe away the tiny hurt. *Talk to me, Chloe.*

"It's a long story," she finally said. "I'm not sure this is the time or the place."

"I see."

"Dinner's about to be served, your mom's just a few yards… I'm sorry."

So was he. It was crazy that she could make him feel in the wrong, but he hated that she'd lost that alluring, unconscious confidence. She was stiff now, uncomfortable, and probably regretting that she'd accepted the dinner invitation. He'd been pushing, but he didn't want to alienate her.

Luckily, between Barb's presence and the natural mellowing properties of food, Chloe had relaxed again midway through dinner. She offered Dylan a slow, appreciative smile; there was a sleepy quality to her expression that made it all too easy to imagine waking up to that face, kissing her good-morning.

"A man who can cook like this," Chloe proclaimed,

"definitely deserves a better kitchen than yours. Something warmer, more interesting, vibrant."

Warm, interesting and vibrant. Did she realize *she* was all three of those things?

Barb set down her fork. "That's right. Dylan mentioned you were going to help him redecorate."

Chloe nodded. "I went and saw the condo last week, made some notes after our meeting. There are some very cool virtual-designer sites where you can check out what different options would look like online."

"Your generation and those computers!" Barb shook her head ruefully. "I can barely check my e-mail. I must have done something wrong, because people say they're sending me stuff I'm not getting."

"Do you want me to look at it for you?" Chloe volunteered. "It could be a simple fix, like your spam filter settings."

"Thank you, that's very kind," Barb said. "Your parents obviously raised you right. Are they still in Mistletoe?"

Chloe started coughing so hard that Barb half rose. Dylan reached around to pat Chloe firmly on the back before his mother panicked and administered the Heimlich.

"Th-thanks." She reached for her drink, her voice scratchy. "Went down the wrong pipe."

I'll bet.

Barb resituated herself in her chair. "I remember once when Dylan was a kid, I thought he was going to choke to death. Some older boy in the neighborhood dared him to see how many marbles he could put in his

mouth, and one accidentally lodged in his throat. Scared
ten years off my life."

"Sorry," he told his mother. He looked back to Chloe.
"It was a stupid thing to do, but sometimes we just lose
our common sense temporarily."

He'd meant it as a subliminal invitation, a way to let
Chloe know that he understood making mistakes and
could forgive. A key difference between him and
Michael Echols. It wasn't Chloe who felt motivated to
share but Barb. She began expounding on some of his
less proud moments, stories that were funny twenty
years later for an outsider but served as a reminder to
Dylan of the vicious cycle he'd created for himself.

He'd been so angry with his impossible-to-please
father that he'd acted out—accepting reckless dares,
taking needless chances on the playgrounds, going for the
laugh in class instead of focusing on difficult-to-process
reading assignments. Naturally, all of these actions had
led to his father labeling him an even bigger loser.

Dylan's appetite disappeared, but since he felt it
would look bad for the chef not to eat his own cooking,
he continued to pick at his food while the ladies finished
their dinners. The three of them worked together to
clear the table and agreed to wait a little while before
dessert. As his mom fired up the coffeemaker, Dylan
and Chloe loaded the dishwasher.

"Were you serious about helping with the e-mail?"
Barb asked hesitantly.

Chloe smiled. "Lead the way."

The PC sat on a desk at the back of the living room.
Dylan turned the television on low volume and checked

scores while the two women behind him discussed different e-mail tools. He liked the way Chloe spoke to his mother. Barb was so far behind the Internet age, it would be easy for a person to sound condescending when answering her questions. It would be equally easy for someone who was an expert in computer technology to unintentionally give too much information, confusing his mother more than she had been in the first place.

Chloe handled everything just right, encouraging the other woman with easy-to-understand, but not dumbed-down, explanations and liberal amounts of praise. Barb blossomed under the friendly tutelage, grasping terms quickly and asking even more questions as they went through drop-down menus and various settings.

Barb laughed at the explanation of "signatures." "Althea Webb ends each e-mail with the oh-so-smug reminder that she won the cake cook-off this year and the year before. Do you know I used to think she typed it every single time?"

Chloe was in the middle of changing the display settings so that everything was larger and easier for Barb to read when his mom gasped. "Heavens, is that the time already? Oh, dear, I've monopolized your whole night! And poor Dylan has to get back to Atlanta in the morning."

His broadcasts weren't until evening, but he did have a station meeting at noon.

"Did you bring your notes and ideas with you?" he asked Chloe.

"Of course." She stood, and he couldn't help watching the line of her body as she stretched. "Is it too late to get started on those?"

"Why don't you leave them with me. We can meet for breakfast on my way out of town to talk about what I might like." This was becoming a habit of his, wanting to know exactly when he could see her again whenever they parted ways.

Unlike other guys in college or even at the high school, he'd veered far away from alcohol, nicotine and any kind of drugs. Not because of parental lectures, but because he wanted to protect himself physically, stay in top condition. Now the man college dorm mates had declared Mr. Squeaky Clean finally had a vice: Chloe Malcolm.

After a brief hesitation, she flashed a genuine smile. "I'd like that."

They all adjourned to the kitchen for coffee and dessert, but his mom had barely filled three mugs before kicking them out of the house.

"It's such a pretty night, the two of you should take your pie out on the porch," she suggested, being about as subtle as Natalie had been when she left him alone with Chloe in the lobby of the reunion hotel.

He remembered the hint of desperation in Chloe's eyes that night. If Natalie had stayed and the three of them had started chatting, would Chloe have relaxed? Would the situation have evolved differently? Or would she have faded into the background while he and Natalie conversed? Maybe her friend had done her a favor, throwing her in the proverbial water and challenging her to come up swimming. Looking at Chloe now, he couldn't imagine this woman panicking over a brief drink with a guy. She was charming.

As it turned out, his mother was right about it being a gorgeous night. He leaned against the porch railing while Chloe took the rocker.

"Don't get stars like this in downtown Atlanta," he admitted.

"Do you miss it?" she asked him. "Living here? I love Mistletoe. I truly do. But sometimes I wonder if I'm missing out, settling."

"For me, Mistletoe was a 'best of times, worst of times' situation. Which is the sum total of what I remember from Lit classes," he joked. "Honestly, I was so focused on ball that I don't remember details about much else. It's only fair to tell you, when I walked into that reunion, Candy Beemis was just a name to me. I didn't have any specific memories or preconceived notions attached to it when I asked you to dinner."

"Really?" She sounded elated. The actual Candy would be clawing his eyes out by now.

For the first time it occurred to him how lucky he'd been to sit with the wrong girl. "Really. I asked you out because you were stunning and I wanted to spend more time with you." He leaned in closer. "You still are, and I still do."

She swallowed, then ran her tongue along her lower lip. He was overcome with a need to know what she tasted like tonight. His Chloe was always full of surprises.

"If it weren't for that policy of yours about not getting involved with clients," he began coaxingly.

"I…" Her gaze was troubled, the internal debate clear in her eyes. "I can't. I want to, but I can't. I should go, Dylan."

Damn.

It wasn't until she'd safely put a few stairs of distance between them that she said, "But I'm looking forward to breakfast tomorrow! We'll talk more then."

He watched her go to her car. It was on the tip of his tongue to call out *Wait, Chloe,* but if he did, he'd never know that she respected him enough, cared about him enough, to tell him the truth herself.

HER FIRST REAL DATE with Dylan Echols. Well, *date* might be too strong a term, but this would be their first meal in public. Chloe's heart thudded madly in her chest. She'd agreed because it was so early in the day and the restaurant was on Dylan's route back to the freeway, practically the outskirts of Mistletoe. Statistically this was the least likely place and time for her to run into people she knew. Still, her mouth was dry and her palms were damp.

How the hell did people commit crimes? If she were even pondering something illegal and happened to pass a police officer, she'd be seized with the uncontrollable urge to turn herself in. *What you're doing to Dylan is a crime. You have to tell him the truth.* She realized that. It had been unfair to ever rationalize that he didn't need to know, even though she'd never dreamed that their acquaintance would continue and evolve.

But she'd let it go on so long. How could she explain what she'd done in a way that didn't make her sound pathological? In a way that didn't make him never want to speak to her again?

"C.J.! Over here." He waved from a back booth. Was

it her guilty conscience, or did his voice boom extra-loud as he signaled her?

She hurried to sit across from him, her back to the restaurant's entrance. "Morning. Before I forget, here are some more URLs I wrote down for you."

As he took the sheet of paper torn from a memo pad, his thumb swirled over her palm, pressing gently against pressure points she hadn't known were there. It shouldn't have been any more sexual than two kids holding hands, but she nearly trembled at the contact. Sitting with him last night on Barb's front porch, Chloe had yearned for more physical contact. She'd bolted in part because she didn't trust herself alone with him. She'd been infatuated with him in high school, but the feelings that had seemed so all-encompassing at the time were nothing compared to the rising desires of an adult woman who'd come to know Dylan more inti-mately.

A curly-haired waitress wearing a faded uniform and funky green horn-rimmed glasses took their orders. After she'd gone, Dylan held up the list Chloe had made of sites and brief notations about each.

"Thanks for these. You sure are going to a lot of trouble."

"Not really." The very fact that Chloe had the time to devote to Dylan and his condo was a glaring neon arrow pointing to her lack of love life. Friends like Natalie spent leisure hours getting ready for dates, going to movies with new boyfriends, shopping for anniversary and Valentine's Day gifts. Chloe spent her free time watching reruns of *House*. She suspected, though, that even if her Web site business kept her so busy that she put in sixty-hour weeks, for Dylan she would have made the time. "Besides, I've been enjoying myself. The site listed at the bottom of the page is entirely too much fun. You can scan in a photo of your room and mess with colors and stuff. The models are crude, but if you're at all a visual person—"

"Oh, I am."

"Most men seem to be," she agreed. "When I did student tutoring—"

He raised an eyebrow and looked as if he might interrupt. Chloe hastily tried to recall what kind of student Candy had been. Plenty of cheerleaders and varsity athletes had been on the honor roll, but the idea of Candy selflessly helping her peers was laughable.

She spoke faster, trying to prevent an interruption even though she'd momentarily lost her train of thought. "I found that guys always absorbed the point faster when they had a diagram or map or illustration. I got really interested in the different ways people learn."

Dylan's expression had changed from questioning to thoughtful, and he nodded.

"It's about knowing how each person gets the best results," she continued. "Like, some people do better with music playing in the background while others need the quiet to focus. Some you joke with to cajole results, others… Well, you get the idea. You'd tell me if I was boring you, right?"

"You're not. Quite the opposite," he said. "I was thinking that you did an amazing job with my mom last night."

Chloe flushed with pleasure, but didn't feel she could take credit for Barb. "She was a quick study. Since my parents moved into the senior living complex, I've started offering short computer tutorials to the residents there. They're not exactly part of the Internet generation, but they still want to be able to access digital pictures of the grandkids and look up occasional recipes on the Web. It's all basic. You could teach it just as well as I could."

He shook his head. "I worry that we fall back on what we know. Whether we want to or not."

"What do you mean?"

"For example…" He stared beyond her, collecting his thoughts. "I've heard children of alcoholics are more likely to *become* alcoholics themselves even though that sounds counterintuitive. You'd think that someone who had witnessed that kind of destruction would be the *last* person to put their own loved ones through it."

"A girl who grew up in my neighborhood used to nag her mother to stop smoking. She even got in trouble once for hiding her mom's cigarettes. Ironically, whenever I see her now, she's smoking outside the Dixieland Diner. Is that what you mean?"

"Exactly," he said grimly.

But Chloe was still confused. What trait was Dylan concerned that he might have picked up, might pass on? The teacher who'd probably made the biggest impact on him was Coach Burton, who was beloved around these parts. And Barb Echols obviously adored her son. Five minutes in the same room with them confirmed that. Chloe frowned, searching her memory banks for any impression of Michael Echols. When she'd brought up the subject of Dylan's father previously, he'd shut her down. She'd assumed that was Dylan's reaction to his father's death, but now she wondered.

"With your interest in learning styles," Dylan asked, "did you ever think about becoming a teacher yourself? Schools can always use good instructors who are attuned to their students and flexible with their teaching styles."

"Actually, I was an education major for all of one semester, not that it mattered since I was only getting started with core classes at the time."

"What made you change your mind?"

The reason sounded so lame she hated to say it, but she owed him the truth about *something*. "Performance anxiety, the idea of standing up in front of an entire class. One-on-one tutoring was a different story. I don't do well in front of crowds. At least, not alone," she added quickly, before he asked any questions about cheerleading. "When I was doing something on a team, the pressure wasn't the same."

That was what had appealed to her about the Academic Decathlon, where they all sat onstage together and could confer over the answers, versus the debate team, which involved individual turns standing at a podium.

"I can understand the comfort of being surrounded by a team," Dylan commiserated. "I think that's been affecting me lately. For more than a decade, I had one team or another. Some of the guys who play for Atlanta still call me, but they have crazy schedules and it's uncomfortable now that I'm a civilian."

She tamped down the impulse to offer herself up as his new team. "I know it will probably never be the same, but do you think that after you've been at the television station longer, you'll develop a similar sense of camaraderie?"

Frowning, he toyed with a packet of sugar. "Not unless they reassign the lead guy to another solar system. He's all ego. He likes himself *way* too much to spare any affection for others, but he specifically dislikes me. On a personal level I don't care. It's not that I want to be his new golfing buddy or anything, but knowing I have to deal with his bs on top of whatever else is going on at work just adds an extra layer of frustration to a job that I'm learning as I go."

"Do you think he feels threatened by you? There was…a girl like that once, who went out of her way to make me feel like an insignificant bug even though all I wanted was to avoid her." Chloe thought of last night, when he'd told her he remembered very little about Candy. It had been a relief that Dylan wasn't attaching any of the woman's negative qualities from years past to Chloe. *Such a hypocrite.* She'd wanted him to associate her with Candy's popularity and charisma, but didn't want to take the blame for any lesser traits. "Natalie insisted she was jealous."

"Maybe. Maybe they're acting out of insecurity." He grinned. "Or maybe they're just asses."

She let out a peal of laughter, his matter-of-fact comment helping to exorcise the last ghosts of adolescent insecurity. All through high school, she'd been unable to think of a comeback, to stand up for herself in a memorable manner. For weeks she'd felt herself changing, evolving. Perversely she half wished someone would insult her so that she could test herself. There was a possibility that now she could react with wit, or at least aplomb.

As long as the person making the cutting comment wasn't Dylan. That—

"Well, hey, there." The friendly female greeting came from mere inches away, and Chloe jumped. "I thought that was you I heard laughing, Ch—"

"Brenna!" *And this is what I get for challenging the universe.* Not that the tall redhead was likely to make an insulting comment, but seeing her here definitely shot Chloe's supposed aplomb all to hell. "Um, have you met Dylan Echols? He's a new client of mine. We were just having a consultation. Dylan, this is Brenna Pierce. She runs her own pet-sitting business. She's Mistletoe's dog whisperer. And cat whisperer. And iguana whisperer."

Chloe knew she should really shut up, having already belabored a mediocre joke, but she was worried that as soon as she stopped talking, Brenna would mention the new Web site mock-ups Chloe had done for her.

Brenna was shaking Dylan's hand, her gaze frankly admiring. "Nice to meet you. I've heard about you, of course. You won't regret hiring this genius. She—"

"Does the fact that you're singing my praises mean you had a chance to look over the design suggestions?" Chloe interjected. She felt rude, panicked and generally nauseous.

Though Brenna looked surprised by the interruption, she nodded. "They're so fantastic my only concern is choosing the right one. All of them had—"

"Positive energy, right? That's my motto!" Did anyone else notice how manic Chloe sounded? "Brenna, Dylan's on his way out of town after breakfast, so we're trying to squeeze this in. Do you want me to call you later about what you'd like me to do?"

"Sure." Brenna was eyeing her as if she thought Chloe had started the day with way too much coffee. Still, she took the hint, turning to go. "It was nice to meet you, Dylan."

I'll need to do some damage control later, Chloe thought. She'd cut Brenna off at least three times in a two-minute conversation and had tried too hard to seem bubbly and unconcerned, veering into deranged. She didn't want to lose Brenna's account.

Glancing back at Dylan, she acknowledged with a sinking sensation in the pit of her stomach that she risked losing something far more valuable.

Chapter Twelve

What did a woman wear to her own downfall? Chloe wondered as she scanned the contents of her closet Saturday at dawn.

Dylan had e-mailed her after his newscast late Thursday night to tell her he was really impressed with some of the notes she'd made regarding his condo. She'd happened to be awake at the time, working on her laptop, so she'd responded immediately. They'd gone from exchanging e-mails to instant messaging—it was almost a little sad how much easier it was for her to express herself through emoticons than face-to-face communication.

Though she'd enjoyed flirting and chatting during her cyber interaction with Dylan—typing was more deliberate than speaking, protecting her from the nervous babbling she was prone to—the computer screen was a lackluster substitute for the man. The more they'd talked, the more she'd wished she was with him. As a teen, she'd bought into the illusion that he was the guy who effortlessly had it all. The reality of him was far more fascinating, an intoxicating puzzle. She wanted to learn all his edges and pieces; everything he'd revealed about himself so far only attracted her more. As a bonus, when she was with him, she'd also been discovering more about who *she* was. The only downside to their time together was that she lived in fear of blurting out the wrong thing, clumsily exposing herself as a liar.

You're living on borrowed time, C.J.

When he'd broached the subject of when she could go with him to look for furnishings and decor, she'd agreed to come to Atlanta today. They'd spend the day shopping then have an early dinner before he had to work. She was resolved that, over dinner, she'd tell him everything and hope for the best. She didn't know if he would forgive her, but if she didn't rectify the situation, she wouldn't be able to forgive herself. One way or the other, this stressful pretense would be ended by tomorrow.

She wasn't sure what they'd be eating, but she hoped it would be good. A girl had high expectations for her last meal.

DYLAN TRIED to keep his eyes on the road, but it was damn difficult with Chloe right next to him, smiling as she reclined her head against the passenger seat. Some of the shorter strands of her layered hair had escaped the barrette, framing her face in soft tendrils.

"Enjoying the convertible?" he asked.

"Mmm. If I had this car, I'd get a job delivering pizzas so I could be driving all the time."

He chuckled. "You'd need to make *really* good tips delivering pizzas if you were going to pay for it, though."

She mock-glared at him over the top her sunglasses. "I'm daydreaming over here. Do not bother me with trivial stuff like reality."

Reality. Was it as clear-cut as he'd once assumed? He'd been angry at her for lying, but there was more C.J. in her than she realized. Whatever her technical job description really was, she'd thrown herself skillfully into the task of suggesting changes for his apartment. Once, he'd assumed that the reality of his injury was that baseball wouldn't be part of his life anymore, but maybe he'd been needlessly limiting his opportunities. On a gorgeous spring day like this, spending his afternoons coaching a bunch of eager kids who loved baseball as much as he did sounded far better than spending six nights a week alongside Grady Medlock. Maybe it was time for both him and Chloe to reexamine what was real and what was malleable.

They reached the interior-decorating warehouse shortly after it opened for the day. While Dylan secured the roof on the car, Chloe fussed with her windblown hair and withdrew a slim tube of lip gloss from her purse.

"I have to know." He watched her put on the shiny layer of color, wanting to kiss it off of her before she'd even finished applying it. "What flavor?"

She blinked, looking startled by the question. "My gloss? Butter pecan."

It made him think of ice cream, the cold sweetness of it melting on his tongue. He hardened at the thought of Chloe against his tongue.

"This cosmetic habit of yours is thoroughly distracting," he told her. "I never know what you'll taste like. It's like dating a woman who wears staid business suits with naughty lingerie underneath. A man could go crazy wondering what's next to her skin. A whisper of ivory silk or a leopard-print thong?"

Chloe's cheeks flamed pink. Had he offended her with the analogy?

After a moment, she smiled. "I'm glad I distract you. Even if it is just my makeup."

He echoed what she'd once said to him in his apartment. "It's not 'just' anything. It's you."

"Thank you for asking me to come with you today," she said. "I...wanted to see you."

"Ditto. And I don't trust myself to decorate the condo by myself. You saw what happened when left to my own devices." He gave an exaggerated shudder, listing some of the feng shui terms she'd taught him. "Elements in conflict, 'secret arrows' every place you look...catastrophe. Save me from myself."

"Don't worry, my assistance is yours as long as you want it." Opening her door, she added softly, "I plan to see this through."

As they crossed the asphalt toward the massive shopping complex, Chloe asked, "So, which of the eight areas do you want to really focus on? Harmonious balance is key, but what are your immediate goals? Wealth? Career? Love? I've...been surprised that there's no girlfriend in your life. There's *not* a girl-friend, right?"

"What the hell kind of guy do you think I am?"

Dylan was incensed. He'd kissed Chloe on multiple occasions—not brief pecks of greeting or farewell, either. Deep soul kisses that had shaken him. He knew players who had "girlfriends" in cities up and down the Eastern Coast, but that had never been his style.

She bridged the gap between them, taking his hand. "I'm sorry. That came out sounding like, I don't know, an accusation. It was just a surprise."

He grunted, not mollified. It was ironic that *she* suspected *him* of being untrustworthy, the kind of guy who would nonchalantly cheat on a woman.

"You're smart and funny and successful," she continued. "The best-looking guy I've ever seen in real life and not on a movie screen. In short, a man some single women would commit unholy acts to meet."

It was difficult to stay angry after praise like that. *She thinks I'm smart?* Rationally he'd known for years that dyslexia was a reading disorder and no reflection of actual intelligence. He was *not* stupid, but he had to remind himself of that routinely.

He held open the heavy glass door for her. "You asked about the area I'm most interested in? Knowledge. With the right knowledge, the information and wisdom to make good decisions, it seems like a lot of the other areas would fall into place."

For instance, should he play it safe and keep his lucrative job in Atlanta, the city that had become home over the past few years? Or throw that away on Coach B.'s whim and return to the place that held some of his ugliest memories?

"Good thinking," Chloe said approvingly. "Of course,

some people feel that too much knowledge can be dangerous. Just ask Adam and Eve."

"I'll take my chances. Ignorance gets good PR, but I don't think it's as blissful as people say."

Chloe had pulled a little memo pad out of her purse. He watched over her shoulder as she jotted down colors that he assumed were applicable to wisdom: yellow, brown and other earthy tones, blue.

"You have that small bookshelf in your living room. We could move it to the knowledge area. And we should find you a great lamp while we're here." She tapped her temple. "For en*light*enment."

"It disturbs me that I can't tell if you're being sincere or if you're just making bad puns."

She gave him a cheeky smile. "Can't I do both? Oh, we should go down that aisle. Vases!"

"I hear *vase* and my only two associations are priceless Ming, which is not in our budget, and girly bud vases. I'm evolved enough that I don't think I have to decorate in leather and moose heads to prove anything, but—"

"Nothing pink and curvy and filled with flowers?" Chloe rolled her eyes. "Duh. Trust me, Echols."

Paradoxically, he did.

AFTER DYLAN'S wholehearted appreciation last time, Chloe had briefly considered bringing another key lime pie with her to dinner at his place. Instead, she'd opted to make the drive to Atlanta with a bottle of white wine. She was going to need a little liquid courage for after they'd eaten, and there was the hope that wine would mellow Dylan before she dropped her bombshell.

While he sautéed the shrimp, she found a corkscrew. *Chardonnay helped get me into this mess, chardonnay can help get me out.*

"Can I pour you a glass of this?" she asked.

"Yes, thanks, but just one. I still have to do my broadcast later." He sounded endearingly disgruntled. "Trust me, I would much rather be here with you than delivering the sports news alongside Grady Medlock."

She clucked her tongue sympathetically. "He's still being a jerk?"

"At this point, jerk would be a step up. He disliked me from the word go, but the hostility's gotten more personal."

"How so?" She settled on a stool, observing him cook for the sheer joy of watching his body move. *Poetry in motion* had always sounded like a cheesy cliché no one but professional ballroom dancers could ever live up to, but Dylan made her rethink her cynicism.

He took his wine, casting her a sheepish glance. "You asked earlier about my being single? I wasn't until recently, right before the reunion as a matter of fact. I was dating a woman named Heidi. She expressed keen interest in helping me maintain friendships with my former teammates, saying that it wasn't healthy to shut myself off from people close to me in a dark time."

Advice that might arguably have some merit to it, but Chloe sensed from his tone that Heidi had not turned out to be entirely altruistic.

"On about three-quarters of our outings, she made sure we met buddies at a club or we double-dated with another Braves player. Then when she found the one she wanted, she broke up with me with a Dear John e-mail telling me to have a nice life."

"That's awful!" Chloe was outraged on his behalf. "The social-climbing witch."

"No argument here. Don't worry, I didn't languish around the condo heartbroken. Mostly I felt dumb for having been so blind. She was clearly manipulative in retrospect, and I must have been brain-dead to get close to her in the first place."

And how is he going to describe me *"in retrospect"?*

When she blanched, he added, "We weren't that close, really. I'm making this sound more important than it was. The reason it has anything to do with Grady is because he has a thing for our makeup artist, who's made it clear she wouldn't mind *my* asking her out—"

"A woman with taste," Chloe decreed.

"But she didn't make an issue out of it before because she knew I was seeing Heidi."

"So now that you're a free agent, she's doing nothing to conceal her feelings, which is getting you even more enmity from Grady?"

"In a nutshell. That must be one of the benefits of being self-employed. No annoying co-workers. No office politics." He reached for the soy sauce and sprinkled a liberal amount over the shrimp and seasoned vegetables steaming in the pan. "Did you know from the beginning you wanted to work by yourself? I'd imagine it could get lonely, not having colleagues to chat with over break or join for drinks at the end of a long week. You miss out on the time-honored tradition of griping about your boss because you *are* your boss."

"It's not lonely." Much. "After all, I have my clients and the people I'm trying to win over as clients. To some extent, I get to control how much I interact with others and choose the days when I want to be a hermit. I'm not very social by nature."

"Not what one would expect to hear from a former cheerleader," he remarked, stirring chopped mushrooms into the stir-fry.

The ginger-scented perfume of dinner cooking would have made her stomach gurgle in happy anticipation if it weren't already tied up in so many knots. She'd planned to tell him tonight. Was it too blunt to respond with, "Yes, but I was never a cheerleader because I'm not the person you've thought I was for the past three weeks—more wine?"

Lord, the poor man would join a monastery. This bimbo Heidi had just done a job on his trust, and now Chloe was going to follow it up with identity theft? At the very least he'd require two forms of ID and a federal background check on the next woman he invited to dinner.

"Ready to eat?" he asked her.

She smiled weakly.

Though she took the first bite just to be polite, the balance of peppers and garlic—a kick without overwhelming the more delicate flavors—soon seduced her. "When I was rattling off your attributes in the parking lot this morning, I forgot to highlight the fact that you can cook."

"Only about four complete meals," he said modestly.

"Maybe, but when they're this good, you can just

keep cooking them over and over and nobody would mind. At least with shrimp and veggies, I can enjoy them without feeling I have to do a marathon on the treadmill. My mother cooks old-school—everything has half a pound of butter or bacon grease added for flavoring. She is perplexed by this wacky, newfangled thing we kids call 'cholesterol.' I mentioned to her that Nat's mom was doing the South Beach Diet, and Mama misinterpreted that to mean Mrs. Young was on vacation."

He grinned at her anecdotes, but there was a serious note in his voice when he asked, "Was it hard growing up with such a generation gap?"

As much as her parents loved her, it seemed ungrateful to complain.

"Plenty of kids had it more difficult than I did, but their age did factor into things," she admitted. "They didn't think they'd have children, and Mama encountered some difficulties with such a late-in-life pregnancy. They were hyperprotective. Not just in a 'your curfew is sundown' kind of way, but hovering. Maybe that's why I'm a self-contained non-people person."

"A lot of kids start to chafe under too many restrictions. Did you ever rebel?"

She wrinkled her nose. "I got highlights once."

"Wild woman."

"I didn't really do the angry teen bit. I loved my parents, and they loved me…almost to the point of neurosis. Right up until middle school I think Mama was afraid that if she let me out of their sight I might have some horrible asthma attack. I used to wonder what it would have been like if I'd had a sibling and wasn't living under the magnifying glass by myself. Being the only recipient for their attention got a little intense sometimes."

"I'm with you on that." Dylan stabbed a shrimp with his fork but didn't lift it to his mouth. He glared at his plate, as if seeing something she couldn't.

"You felt smothered, too?" She actually thought Barb had done a laudable job making sure Dylan and Chloe had some time alone the other night. Of course, Barb had also suggested pulling out baby pictures and sports mementos. *Maybe I shouldn't have encouraged her.*

But Dylan was shaking his head, making it clear she'd misdiagnosed the problem. "My father was ashamed of me," he stated calmly. "Being the only recipient for his disapproval could definitely get intense."

Her knee-jerk reaction was to insist that there was no way his father had been ashamed of him—the man would have to have been crazy. Half the town of Mistletoe was glowingly proud of Dylan. How could his own flesh and blood be so unnaturally different? But beneath Dylan's neutral expression was a gravity that made it clear he believed his words and hadn't arrived at the conclusion lightly.

Her second reaction was to pronounce his father an idiot, but it seemed wrong to speak ill of the dead.

"I'm dyslexic," Dylan said by way of explanation.

"I didn't know that!"

He smiled wryly. "Is there any reason you should have?"

"No, of course not." It had been a silly response to his declaration, but it seemed bizarre when she knew so many details about him—his favorite dessert, his baseball stats, even what his bedspread looked like— not to know something that had obviously been a defining factor in his life.

"School was a struggle for me," he said.

She experienced a surge of guilt, recalling her own feelings of adolescent inadequacy and her misplaced certainty that people like Dylan Echols had it easy. If nothing else, tutoring Natalie and seeing her friend's tears of frustration over math should have disabused her of that notion.

"If you were struggling, it didn't show. Other students, even teammates of yours, had noticeable difficulties in some of their classes. Or with girlfriends. Or with their parents divorcing or losing jobs or whatever. You always seemed to have everything so together."

His laugh was hollow. "Then I'm definitely not who you thought I was."

She caught her bottom lip between her teeth. Was now the time to tell him she wasn't who he thought, either? It seemed tactless to interrupt what he was trying to share with her to make her own revelation. She was incredibly touched that he would tell him about his dyslexia and his father, which were both clearly difficult subjects for him.

"You think your dad was bothered by your dyslexia?"

Dylan pushed his plate away. "I think my father saw me as an extension of himself. Mom said he was so proud for the first three years. He had his own boy, a strapping lad! When I pitched a no-hitter, he lived vicariously. But any time I got in trouble or flunked a spelling test or got sent to the principal's office in grade school because I was making jokes, I was an embarrassment to him."

"Then I feel sorry for him for the way he screwed up having a decent relationship with you." And now, with Michael Echols dead, it was too late. She suddenly felt motivated to call her parents on the way home tonight, just to say she loved them.

"As I get older and look back with more perspective, I try not to take it personally. I don't think he was kind in general," Dylan said. "He ran roughshod over Mom, but she mostly learned to let him have his way and keep the peace. I wasn't so diplomatic."

Recalling his earlier question about her own youthful rebellions—of which there were none—she hazarded a guess. "You sought out trouble?"

"Until seventh-grade baseball," he affirmed. "I knew that if I got suspended, no more playing. After middle school was high school and Coach Burton, who kept me on the straight and narrow. He's the one who told me the great Nolan Ryan was dyslexic."

Even if Dylan's career had been cut short, it sounded as though baseball had saved him. It gave her a new appreciation for organized sports.

"I don't know why I'm telling you all this," he said. "It sounds like a poor-me sob story, doesn't it?"

"No! And I'm honored that you're confiding in me." Everything he said made her admire him even more.

"You just really impressed me with what you said

over breakfast the last time I saw you, about how teaching kids depends on finding the right way to get through to them. That a student isn't stupid simply because he doesn't digest information the same way other pupils do. I wish more people had expressed that sentiment to me when I was younger."

So did she. "People can be cruel in what they say, even if it's not intentional."

He shrugged. "More than people insinuating I was dumb, what really bothered me were the times I actually felt that way. Making bad judgment calls, stupid mistakes. But I guess everyone has their share of those, right?"

Lord, yes.

She wrestled with the desire to tell him about her own lapse of judgment when she'd let him believe she was someone else. But juxtaposed with her desperation to own up was the dawning realization of how she might make him feel. Would he blame himself for not seeing through her pitiful attempts at deception? He'd called himself "brain-dead" for not seeing Heidi more clearly. Chloe had seen the banked pain in his eyes when he talked about his father. She never wanted to do anything that brought him that same pain.

She'd thought tonight was going to be her downfall, and she was partially right. After a day of joking with him and sharing opinions at the decorating warehouse and an intimate evening of dinner and conversation, she had fallen for him completely. But she couldn't tell him the truth. Chloe would rather finish this "job" and walk away from him than do anything that made him doubt his own intelligence and self-worth.

Chapter Thirteen

"It was such a nice surprise that you called last night and were able to join us for Sunday brunch," Rose Malcolm said, smiling at Chloe from the sink. "We haven't seen much of you in the past couple of weeks."

Chloe carried the last of the plates to the counter and reached for a sponge so that she could help her mother wash the dishes while her father read the Sunday paper in the next room. The Malcolms' new place included a dishwasher, but Rose never used it since it didn't get rid of every spot on the glasses and silverware, failing to meet her exacting standards.

"I'm sorry I haven't been around, Mama. I've been busy with work, but also some other things." She cleared her throat. "In fact, I've been meaning to ask you…is it all right if I make some changes to the house? Nothing big! I'm not planning to knock down any walls or anything. I just thought maybe I could do some redecorating." Ferreting out information and studying color groups for Dylan had inspired her.

Rose tilted her head, looking confused. "Your father

and I gave you that house permanently, dear. You may do with it as you please. Fix it up, sell it, anything you deem acceptable."

"Thank you, Mama."

"If you want to pick out some new colors and textures, I'm sure you'll do a lovely job. June Albright had me over for tea yesterday and showed me that Web site you did for her grandson. I don't understand any of what you actually do, but you have a good eye."

Gratitude swelled within her, not just for her mother's words of praise but for having two loving, healthy parents. In all those moments when she'd longed to be someone other than she was, she'd lost sight of just how many blessings Chloe Ann Malcolm actually had.

"You know," Rose added with a sidelong glance, "June has another grandson who's in his early thirties and is still single. Beau, I believe his name is. She said she'd be happy to introduce you sometime."

Chloe had discovered that this was the biggest drawback to her parents moving into the community at the seniors' complex—lots of retired people with time on their hands who all wanted grandchildren and great-grandchildren. It was a matchmaker's colony. "I know who Beau is. Our paths haven't crossed directly, but he seems like a nice man."

He just wasn't Dylan Echols.

Rose beamed. "Does this mean I should tell June to set something up?"

"Oh, no. I'm flattered she thought of me, but…"

"Is this because you're too 'busy'? Or is it just because you're shy? I know meeting people hasn't always been easy for you."

"Actually, Mama, I *have* met someone. Just recently. We're not dating, but I care about him."

Her mother's expression lit up. "Well, don't stop there! Tell me more about him, dear."

"He's my age, successful, takes good care of his mother. We may never be more than friends," Chloe warned, "but it probably isn't fair to go out with Beau until I know more."

"I see." Rose dipped a plate in the soapy water. "And if a relationship does develop, you will bring him over so that we can meet this young man, won't you?"

"Absolutely." Not that she could ever bring Dylan to meet her parents if she were operating under an assumed name.

She thought of yesterday, how much fun they'd had shopping and pointing out why they liked or disliked certain items, how he'd taken her breath away with his candor over dinner.

With their relationship progressing, what choice did she have other than to tell him the truth? They could never go any further if she didn't. Three weeks ago, she never would have believed she could have a relationship with Dylan Echols. But now she knew they were far more compatible than she had ever imagined, knew how special he was. She might even be falling in love with the proud, imperfect man he'd become, not the boy she'd hardly known.

She began drying the plates and bowls that were

already clean. "Mama? When you married Daddy, how did you know for certain that you loved him?"

"Love?" Rose stopped what she was doing, glancing covertly at the doorway into the den before looking back at Chloe. "Now don't take this the wrong way, dear, because I definitely love your father and vice versa, but we cultivated those feelings over decades together. It was never in my personality to get married on an impetuous romantic whim. That was Jane's style, God rest her soul."

Not wanting to be argumentative, Chloe refrained from pointing out that she didn't think her aunt had ever regretted her impulsive elopement. Chloe understood that her mother had always been slightly alarmed by the reckless way her younger sister had lived her life. Rose was speaking more out of that habitual fear than criticism.

"Your father and I met through our families. We were both living in Mistletoe with no plans to go anywhere else, eventually joined the same church. He had a steady job at the carpet plant and was on track to go into management there. I married him because he was a decent man and showed every sign of being a stable provider.

"Romantic love can be fleeting, deceptive. People shouldn't act on that alone as motivation," Rose cautioned. "It was always a great comfort to me, when you were in high school and other teenage girls were spending their Friday nights doing who-knows-what out at Mistletoe Cove, that you were too practical to get carried away."

The fact that so few boys had been interested in dating her also had something to do with it. "That's me, practical Chloe." Yes, she'd been the smart girl with straight A's, but on rare occasions, late at night, she'd wondered what it would be like to be the exciting girl with the illicit hickey.

Rose patted her cheek. "Don't worry about falling in love, dear. Just do what you've always done and follow your brain. I rest easier knowing you're too sensible to make the kind of spur-of-the-moment mistake other people spend so much time regretting."

Chloe managed a feeble smile but kept her mouth shut. Practical Chloe she may well be, but her mom had evidently never met C.J.

CHLOE'S PARENTS had raised her to fear consequences. As a girl, she'd believed that in life, as in fairy tales, wicked deeds were punished and the true-hearted heroine would always get her happy ending. It was one of the many reasons she had never liked Candy Beemis, who proved a glaring exception to the rule. But now Chloe's universe had gone topsy-turvy. She'd performed the single most duplicitous act of her life and was being rewarded at every turn.

Monday morning, she woke up to a brief but entertaining e-mail from Dylan. He recounted an anecdote about a run-in with Grady, exaggerated for comedic effect, and how much he was dreading a PR event with the man later in the week. He also mentioned that he would be having lunch in Atlanta with Coach Todd Burton and that he'd been thinking about her. Then he left a message on her answering machine Tuesday to say that he'd scheduled a pickup for some of the furniture they'd decided he should replace, that he was looking forward to seeing the "new and improved" apartment when the pieces they'd ordered started to arrive later in the week, that he'd had a really inspiring lunch with Coach B....and he was still thinking about her. A lot.

On Wednesday evening, she hit the treadmill, showered and put on her pajamas early. She grabbed her laptop and decided to spend the rest of the night working from the comfort of her bed—one of the major perks of her job. First she checked her e-mail, experiencing an irrational twinge of disappointment when there was no further correspondence from Dylan. *Get a grip.* Was she so needy that she had to hear from him every day? Of course not! She was a modern independent woman.

She was working on a dummy sample home page for Rachel Waide's photography business when the phone rang. Tearing her attention away from an annoying spacing error, she reached for the phone. "Hello?"

"Hey." His voice came through the line, putting him right there in the room with her. "It's Dylan."

A wide smile had spread across her face as soon as he'd said the first word, the kind of grin that was so big it threatened to make her face hurt. "This is a nice surprise."

He laughed, a touch self-consciously. "Is it? I don't see how it could be all that surprising since I feel like I've been stalking you."

"It's not officially stalking until you've started keeping a journal of details about the other person. And, of course, the all-important collection of candid photos and/or news clippings," she teased.

"Ah, good to know." He paused, his tone less flippant when he spoke again. "I have to go to work soon, but I wondered if you had a few minutes to talk?"

"Absolutely." She set the laptop to hibernate and put it aside, wiggling around until she was more comfortable against the pillows.

"Great. Because I'd value your opinion on something."

"Decorating issue?" She eyed the stack of feng shui books on her nightstand.

"Career advice," he corrected. "I told you that I had a very informative lunch with the coach yesterday. I keep tossing it over in my mind. He wants me to interview for the coaching position at the high school. I have my bachelor's degree, but to work at a public school, there are some extra courses I'd need to take. If they were interested in hiring me, I'd probably start as an assistant to Asbury while I worked on rounding out my teaching qualifications, then I'd take over when he retires."

"Sounds like you and Coach B. have given this substantial thought," she said.

"That's a nice way to describe my obsessing over it. I have to tell you, going back to school in any way, shape or form does not fill me with joy."

"I can see where that would be one of the cons for you," she empathized. "On the pro side, you should see yourself when you talk about what baseball meant to you as a teen. I know most of the kids who play ball here in Mistletoe are never going to get a shot at it professionally, but it can still make a major difference in their lives while they're part of the program. *You* could make a major difference."

"You sound so sure of that." He, on the other hand, did not. "I worry about my father's legacy. I still hear his voice in my head. I don't want to pass that on to some other poor kid, lashing out at him because he can't even hit a meatball pitch or because he went for the glory of tagging out a runner instead of tossing it to a closer teammate. Everyone makes mistakes, and I'm not sure I have Coach Burton's tolerance and patience. He always made you want to try again and do better, to prove he was right to believe in you, but there are bad coaches out there, too, who can really sap your will to play."

She hesitated. Giving the pat assurance that he'd do a great job would be easy for her to say, but it wouldn't really address his fears. "I understand why you're worried, but I think you're overlooking an important factor. You're not fully taking into account Coach B.'s legacy. You have so much respect and affection for him that you're far more likely to follow in *his* footsteps than your father's. And because you're already hyperaware of the importance of being firm without being cruel, I suspect you'll be extra vigilant, weighing all your words and actions more than most do."

"Thank you." He exhaled, relief clear in his voice. "That was exactly what I needed to hear."

Her heart thumped with excitement. "So you think there's a chance you might really do it?"

"I'm going to set up an interview with the school board," he decided. "What happens after that, we'll just have to see."

Dylan might be moving back to Mistletoe! She could

conceivably see him *every day*. Chloe hung up the phone and tucked her knees to her chest, grinning in the lamplight as she hugged herself. She was euphoric.

For all of two seconds.

If he lived here, he'd know who she was. The only reason she'd been able to keep her secret was because it had been a long-distance fib. She'd worried about hurting him, but at this point, it was inescapable. All that she could control was whether he found out because she herself took deliberate action, rather than his finding out from someone else. She had to tell him. The sooner, the better.

So how was she going to do it?

She'd been aware for years that she was a nervous babbler around people she didn't know well—it was one of the reasons she tried to keep her mouth shut whenever possible. Better a stranger judge her aloof than think of her as the Crazy Woman Who Can't Shut Up. Could she make Dylan understand that, when she'd seen him that first night, her mouth and brain had disconnected from each other and stuff had just started spilling out?

Yeah, that was going to make up for lying to the man for weeks on end. She'd just tell him her mouth had gone on autopilot, and he'd tell her he understood completely. People invented new identities all the time. *In the witness protection program!*

Disgusted with herself, she whipped back the covers, unbuttoning her pajama top as she crossed the room. Whatever she told him, he deserved to hear it face-to-face. And the drive to Atlanta would give her time to figure out what to say.

Chapter Fourteen

Surprised to hear anyone knocking at this hour, Dylan went to the front door. More than once the easygoing but chronically forgetful tenant from the second floor had locked himself out and come up here to call friends who had a spare key. The guy owned a cell phone but often neglected to keep it charged. Dylan glanced through the security hole and found not his goateed neighbor but Chloe. She must have jumped in her car scant minutes after they'd hung up.

He opened the door and as soon as he got a good look at her tearstained face, ravaged with grief and guilt, he knew exactly why she was there. *Thank God.* She was confessing! He sent up a heartfelt prayer of gratitude. The ludicrous game that had spun out of control was at an end. He itched to pull her to him and rain kisses over her. He'd held himself in check until now, and his control was strained to the breaking point.

Her presence here couldn't have happened at a better time. Earlier tonight, she'd been the only person he wanted to turn to, the person who'd given him the exact input he'd needed, and he'd realized just how much he'd fallen for her.

"Dylan." She took in his partially dressed state of slacks and undershirt. "I hope I'm not bothering you, but—"

"C.J." *Chloe*. He tugged her into his arms, tilting her face up to him. She cared about him enough to share the difficult truth, had driven all this way in the middle of the night. He was delirious with the need to touch her, the need to comfort her.

What seemed like a lifetime ago, he'd wanted to see her break down. Now all he wanted to do was kiss away her tears.

"I am so glad to see you," he breathed, letting go of her just long enough to shut the door behind her.

"You might not be for long," she warned.

"No, don't say that." He shook his head. "I'll always be glad to see you. My heart does this stutter like it's suspended in time for that second when I first lay eyes on you. It happened when I saw you in that hotel lobby and every time since."

Unable to stop himself—not *wanting* to stop himself—he drew her back to him and kissed her. He was better at articulating his feelings that way. At the last minute, he made an attempt to slow down, softening the kiss so that he didn't pounce on her like a starving man presented with a buffet.

Instead, he nipped at her lower lip, sucking gently. She hadn't bothered with makeup before her late-night drive, and it was the first time he'd ever kissed her when she wasn't wearing lip gloss. She tasted like…Chloe, the most erotic flavor he'd ever sampled.

Fingers meshed in her hair, he speared his tongue into the soft heat of her mouth. She whimpered, but it was clearly not a sound of protest since she was frantically wriggling closer. He kissed his way down the column of her throat, murmuring against her skin. "You are so beautiful. And I want you so badly."

Joining their mouths once again, he cupped her breast through the cotton of her T-shirt, and she arched into his palm. Then he lowered his hand beneath the hem, skimming over the sensitive skin of her midriff.

Although it had never been a question he felt compelled to ask anyone before, he heard himself say, "Do you want me, too?" Even with all the physical evidence before him, there was the faintest note of uncertainty in his tone.

She swallowed. "God, yes. You… I…"

When the tenderness in her expression gave way to apprehension, he laid a finger over her deliciously bare lips. Now that they were finally body to body and he knew without a doubt he could trust her, he couldn't bear to lose this moment. "Shh. It's okay, you don't have to put it into words." He might not be able to throw his best fastball anymore, but physical therapy had left him more than able to scoop her up and carry her toward the bedroom. Since a charitable organization had come by to collect some of the pieces he'd be replacing, such as his nightstand, the bedroom was starker than it had been before, making the bed such a focal point of the room that it might as well have neon flashing arrows over it.

But, of course, arrows angled at him would be negative chi, and Dylan was feeling *extremely* positive about life right now.

As soon as he'd set her on the foot of the bed, he tugged off his shirt. Then he reached for hers, removing it so quickly it was as if the fabric obligingly disintegrated. She sucked in a breath, causing her chest to swell in the lacy cups of a pale pink bra. Her skin was pale, too, smooth and exquisitely delicate. Pressing her against the mattress, he dropped kisses across her shoulder and collarbone, his fingers tracing circles over her abdomen.

"I came here to tell you something," she said.

He glanced up, meeting her gaze. "If it was to tell me that you think you're falling in love with me, the feeling is mutual."

She froze, her eyes widening. "It is? You are?"

Feeling far shier than he had when he'd first done this at sixteen, he nodded. She plunged her fingers through his hair, pulled him closer and kissed him fervently, putting her whole heart into it. He kissed her back, realizing that for the first time in his life, he had his whole heart to give. He'd always dated, but baseball had been his first love, demanding so much time and concentration. And after confiding in her the other night about his childhood, he felt he'd cleared out emotional cobwebs that had kept him from experiencing everything so vividly before.

His previous encounters with women had been grainy and blurred; Chloe was hi-def.

Kissing the slope of her breast, he was pleased to discover that her bra had a front clasp. He flicked it open with the enthusiastic awe of a boy unwrapping a long-awaited birthday present. Propping himself on an elbow, he simply admired her for a second.

She wiggled, and he wasn't sure if she was trying to press their bodies closer because she missed the contact or because she was trying to shield herself from his gaze. "I'm not going to be able to talk to you naked," she fretted.

"Excellent, then we'll talk later."

"But, I—"

"It will be okay." He rubbed a thumb over one pebbled nipple. "It will be more than okay, I promise." Then he lowered his head to take her in his mouth, and her words faded to gasps.

He managed to get them both undressed, although it was difficult to concentrate on the button and zipper of his slacks with Chloe raking her nails lightly over his chest and running her tongue across his earlobe. The shell-pink panties she wore were silky, but she was far silkier beneath them, hot and wet to his touch. He pressed his thumb against her, almost lost control himself when he slid his finger into her. Her head dropped back, her breathing erotically ragged. Watching her climax was humbling.

"You are magnificent," he whispered, kissing her and tasting salt on her skin.

It wasn't until he'd rolled on a condom that he realized the fundamental flaw in his interrupting her earlier. As he sheathed himself in the welcoming tightness of her body, he regretted not being able to call her by name. But if they had to stop *now* for questions and explanations... So her name became a wordless chant in his mind as he pulled back and slowly thrust. He slid his hands over the sleek muscles of her toned legs, which she'd wrapped around his hips.

Dylan lost himself inside her. Inside her eyes and her touch and the way she quivered around him. When she came a second time, she locked her arms and legs around him and cried his name. It sent him over the edge.

Afterward, he felt dazed and dumbstruck. He wasn't even sure how much time had passed, although he knew it was late, when Chloe prompted, "Dylan?"

He yawned, his eyes feeling as heavy as two-ton weights. "Hmm?"

Her own voice sounded sleepy but determined. "Are you awake?"

"Definitely not. Best dream of my life," he said, hugging her.

"Can we talk?"

"In mornin'," he mumbled. His last waking thought was of how lucky he'd been to go to that reunion.

CHLOE WOKE INSTANTLY, jolted from a dreamless sleep. She felt as if she'd been unconscious for years—a naked and slightly sore Rip Van Winkle. Sunlight spilled around the edges of a window shade in an unadorned window. They'd picked out new window treatments Dylan planned to install this weekend. *Dylan!*

Emotion spasmed through her, intense joy at what had taken place between them and daunting trepidation that she still hadn't told him who she really was. Last night she'd said she couldn't talk to him in the nude, a tactical error on her part. Perhaps she had a better shot of helping him work through his understandable anger if there weren't a lot of clothes between them.

"Hello?" She listened for the sound of water running or rummaging in the kitchen. "Dylan?"

Her voice echoed in the empty apartment. Confused, she wrapped the sheet around herself, trailing it behind her as she explored the place. No mistake about it, he wasn't here.

But on the otherwise tidy kitchen counter sat a gold key on a Braves keychain and a note. It took her a second to adjust to his handwriting, definitely the kind described as chicken-scratch.

C,

Had to leave early—damn PR thing. Couldn't wake you. Stay as long as you want. Lock up when you go.

Call you,

D.

For no good reason, despair filled her. She had next to no experience with mornings after, but while some of them had been awkward, this was the only one that had featured a jotted memo instead of the actual guy. *What were you expecting, a sonnet?* Well, no. But "last night was the most magical experience of my life" would have been nice. Or at the very least, "love, Dylan." Even "fondly" would have been an improvement to the terse letter.

She found herself chewing on her thumbnail and she impatiently dropped her hand. Had he really tried to wake her? Sneaking off in the light of day with a vague promise of calling later sounded like the horror stories she'd heard from girlfriends on the unreliability of guys. *Stop being so insecure. He's never given you any reason not to believe him.* In point of fact, she was the liar in this relationship.

Oh God. She'd slept with a man under false pretenses. How had she let it get that far? Images played through her mind—the way he'd looked at her, spoken to her, touched her. Okay, she knew *how* she'd let it happen; she just wished she'd told him the truth first. Now it was going to be doubly hard. She wasn't even sure when he would be back. Earlier in the week he'd mentioned a publicity function at Turner Field, some sort of all-day event each of Channel Six's personalities were expected to attend. Should she—

The phone cut into the silence, making her jump. She didn't answer, figuring that if Dylan wanted to talk to her, he would have tried her cell. A moment later, his voice filled the condo as he told the caller no one was available right now and instructed them to speak at the beep.

"Hey, dude, it's Nick. Ran into Coach at the bakery and he said it looks as if you're gonna apply. It will take someone special to fill his cleats—you'd be perfect. And I called 'cause my curiosity is killing me—what happened with Chloe? Next time you're in town, holler. You, me and Shane will hang out."

What happened with Chloe?

Nausea swamped her so hard she almost fell, grabbing the edge of the counter to steady herself. He knew! She'd racked her brain trying to figure out how to tell him, and he knew. *Had known,* last night when he'd made love to her. When he'd interrupted her multiple times as she tried to spit out the truth. Not only did he know, he'd told his buddies about it.

She pressed her hands to her eyes. Had this been a lark for him, or something more sinister like revenge?

While she had been dying a thousand deaths over her deception, had he been planning all along to seduce her and teach her a lesson? *Boy, did you let yourself get seduced!* They'd gone from first base to scoring pretty damn quickly. She was ashamed of herself. *I should have told him sooner, should have tried harder...*

True. But did that excuse his yukking it up with friends? Nick wanted an update. Would Dylan give him one? Would she become the grown-up equivalent of locker-room talk? She'd considered Nick a friend once, or at least a friendly acquaintance. Then again, he'd dated Candy Beemis, hung out with a lot of the same popular kids who'd sneered at her and called her Klutzy Chloe. Were they all laughing again? She knew she'd screwed up, but she hated that instead of just calling her a liar, Dylan had turned her into the butt of an old joke that hadn't been funny ten years ago and wasn't now.

The difference was, she was no longer a mild-mannered seventeen-year-old who lacked the backbone to stand up for herself. She was furious. *What would C.J. do?*

Looking around the kitchen with the strategic gaze of a woman scorned, she glimpsed the business card they'd picked up from the decorating warehouse, where

Dylan had introduced her as his decorator. The card was pressed to the fridge with a magnet from a local Chinese delivery place. She retrieved it, staring at the promise that they provided the essentials for every design taste and philosophy. With an idea beginning to take shape in her mind, she slid the card into her purse—which also contained the uncashed check she'd planned to return as a symbolic gesture once she'd told him who she wasn't.

Chloe scanned her mental library of everything she'd read about feng shui. She'd promised to help Dylan use the guidelines for more positive energy, after all, and she'd always excelled at book learning. Now she was going to take a bunch of suggestions and get Dylan Echols all the good chi he deserved.

IF GRADY MEDLOCK HAD made one smart-ass comment about how goodwill events didn't involve being abrupt with the public…well, he would have been absolutely right. Dylan tried to tamp down his impatience, but he was dying to get out of there. It had nothing to do with being in this stadium, where he'd once played and hadn't been able to imagine anything more thrilling than the roar of the crowd and the certainty that came with the perfect pitch that the batter would miss. Instead, it was all about the woman he'd kissed goodbye that morning. Although she'd snored through that, he recalled, grinning inwardly.

When he'd first awakened, a naked Chloe in his arms, he'd entertained calling in sick. But if his interview with the school board went well, he was about to spit in the faces of those who had pulled strings and lobbied for him to have the Channel Six job. The very least he could do was honor his final commitments.

Then he would be free to go home to Mistletoe, to baseball and to Chloe.

The day passed in an eternity of small talk and autographs. He stole a fifteen-minute break for a late lunch and tried Chloe's cell number, but there was no answer. Since all the words that came to mind seemed inadequate, he didn't bother with a message. Finally, he was free to go…and sit in Atlanta traffic. He glared at the cars moving so slowly they might as well be parked. What sadistic fan of irony had deemed this "rush" hour?

When he got home, he raced up the stairs two at a time, knowing even as he did so that it was foolish. There was a good chance she wouldn't even be there. It had been a gift that she'd shown up last night, but he couldn't expect her to put her life on hold and sit around waiting for him all day. It was a sweet fantasy, though, the idea that he would come home to find Chloe.

Maybe even in bed? He had dyslexia and a bum rotator cuff. A naked Chloe reclining on his mattress would be the perfect way for karma to make it all up to him.

"Hello?" He was calling out even before he had the door fully open. "Is any—"

What in the name of all that was holy and good had happened to his apartment?

His gaze was bouncing around like a caffeinated pre-schooler, moving so quickly that he couldn't really process everything he was seeing. Such as that one section of the room where there was so much purple and gold that it looked like Mardi Gras had thrown up in the corner.

Purple and gold. She'd said that those colors were associated with wealth, hadn't she? In the "romance" area were fuzzy pink heart-shaped pillows resting on his couch. And a red throw rug with hideous naked cavorting cupids!

He stomped through the apartment. Was this her idea of a prank? Her way of saying she hadn't found last night as satisfying as he had? In the kitchen, next to his spice rack, now hung a freakishly ugly still life of fruit in a bowl. It looked like it had been painted by a toddler with anger-management issues. Right after he noticed the gilded mirror she'd somehow affixed over top his stove, he realized that the business card from his fridge was missing. Surely she wouldn't…

With a sinking feeling low in his belly, he wondered if he would still be getting that delivery from the warehouse tomorrow with the new odds and ends they'd picked out or if a certain *interior decorator* had changed the order?

He hurried to the phone, not sure yet if he intended to call the warehouse first or Chloe, to demand an explanation and offer the chance to grovel for forgiveness. This wasn't bad taste—her own home might not have been a bastion of high design, but it hadn't been Roy's House of Tacky, either—this was deliberate. He remembered how he'd told her he didn't want anything too effeminate or busy. Her exact words had been *trust me*.

Like a jackass, he had. Repeatedly.

It wasn't until he reached for the receiver that the blinking red light on the answering machine finally cut through his murderous preoccupation. He stabbed the button, hoping to hear Chloe's voice tell him that it was all a belated April Fool's joke. Instead Nick Zeth's voice boomed out. Dylan was about to hit the stop button, his potential job in Mistletoe currently the last thing on his mind, but froze when he heard his friend ask "What happened with Chloe?"

Oh, hell.

She'd heard the call. It was the only reason—besides her being psychotic, and possibly color-blind—for her going nuts like this after what had been one of the best nights of his life. For a millisecond, he was tempted to blame Nick for this fiasco, but Dylan wasn't a moron. How could he fault Nick when he was the only person in this entire mess who'd been entirely honest?

Still, Chloe had a lot of nerve saddling up a high horse under the circumstances. He glared at the blinking lights that now hung from his bedroom ceiling but stopped when he started to develop a headache. *When I get my hands on her...*

No time like the present. He turned off the lights and left in such a hurry that he nearly forgot to lock the door. Of course, he reminded himself, anyone stealing from his apartment in its current condition would be doing him a favor.

ALTHOUGH SHE'D FELT grimly satisfied when she'd left Dylan's apartment, impressed with her own speedy efforts, Chloe couldn't sustain the feeling all the way back to Mistletoe. Had she stood up for herself, or merely thrown a peevish tantrum involving gilt light fixtures and cheap fabrics? Had she only made a bad situation worse?

You fell in love and got your heart broken. Did it *get* much worse? Her mother may have been right about the emotion. Chloe never should have trusted in it, especially when it had been formed on such a shaky basis. Trying to have a relationship with Dylan after she'd lied to him was like building a house on quicksand, then having the gall to look surprised when it turned out to be an unlivable disaster.

She wished she hadn't fallen in love. She wished she hadn't lied. She wished she'd never even gone to that stupid reunion.

By the time she got home, she was sniffling back a torrent of tears. She'd called Natalie earlier, but her friend had a consultation with a bride today and had sworn to come by the house as soon as humanly possible. Chloe kicked off her shoes and went straight for her freezer, wondering if it was possible to literally drown your troubles in ice cream. *Death by fudge-mint ripple.* There were worse ways to go.

When the frantic pounding came at her front door, she was relieved. She put down the spoon she'd been using to eat straight from the carton. *Thank goodness, Nat's come to save me from myself.*

She swung open the door, and all the ice cream she'd downed threatened to come back up. "Oh, crap."

"Nice to see you, too." Dylan raised his eyebrows, taking a step forward so that she had no choice but to retreat, letting him inside. "Chloe Malcolm, I presume?"

Chapter Fifteen

Stand your ground, Chloe admonished herself. As if she had a choice—her legs were trembling too badly to make a run for it. "It's not like my identity comes as a surprise to you," she retorted accusingly. "You knew."

He crossed his arms over his chest and nodded sharply. "I knew. No thanks to you. A guy could grow old waiting for you to develop a conscience."

The truth in his words stung. Hadn't she tried multiple times to gear up her courage and face what she'd thought would be her biggest humiliation ever? That had been before the embarrassment of this morning, realizing that she'd made love to Dylan when he...

"I tried to tell you last night," she said in a weak stab at self-defense. "You didn't let me get the words out."

He had the grace to look chagrined.

"Did you deliberately interrupt?" she demanded. "Just so you could keep stringing me along for your own amusement?"

"Stringing you along? Don't make me the bad guy

here! I've been patiently waiting. Ever since the night of the reunion."

She felt the blood drain from her face. "You've known since then?"

"You're not a gifted liar. But what gave it away was running into Candy Beemis downstairs. Once I'd seen both of you, I couldn't figure out how I ever made the mistake in the first place."

Because Candy was so much more glamorous? Chloe flinched, turning toward the living room where she could at least sag against the sofa for support. "I'm sorry. I never meant to lie to you. I know that doesn't change what I've done, but it wasn't intentional. And if you'd given me half a chance, I would have made this apology *last night!* What the hell was that?"

"Well, if I have to explain it to you…"

Was he trying to make a joke about what had happened, or was he just being sarcastic? Either way, she didn't appreciate it. She glared in wordless reproach.

His expression grew more earnest. "I've been trying so hard not to touch you. No matter how badly I wanted you. And then I finally had you in my arms, passionate and—"

"So you were more interested in getting laid than hearing the truth?" Tears pricked her eyes as she remembered their fiery encounter. Where had her own willpower been? *She* could've said no. In theory.

In reality, she wasn't sure she had the iron discipline to walk away from the temptation of making love with Dylan Echols. But what had been beautiful at the time, magical even, now seemed like her biggest mistake of all.

"Did you tell your buddies about last night?" she asked hollowly, wondering if she was going to become a laughingstock in town. None of the gossips in high school had ever had ammunition this juicy to use against her.

"Like you didn't tell Natalie?"

"Because I was seeking advice!" Her voice rose, quavering. "Because I felt horrible—"

"You deserved to feel bad. Do you know how it made *me* feel when I realized I'd been duped?"

That had been what she couldn't face, making him feel foolish. "I am sorry, Dylan. If I could go back, I would erase it all, I really would."

"All of it?" Until his voice suddenly dropped to a murmur, she hadn't realized they'd been yelling at each other.

She wanted to curl up under her comforter and cry. The worst part was that she *liked* who she'd become during the past month. She'd taken too much pleasure in Dylan's company and discovering the C.J. side of herself. Now it was all muddled together, mired in guilt and confusion.

"You deserved an apology," she said tiredly. "For my lying to you, for what I did to your apartment. And you have it. I'm truly sorry. If I could take it all back, I would. But since I can't…please just go."

He clenched his jaw, somehow looking angrier now than when he'd first arrived. "If you're sure that's what you want?"

Unable to look at him, she nodded.

He didn't say a word as he crossed back to the front door. But he stopped there. "Then you're a coward."

Her head jerked up. "What?"

"I thought…I thought we had something special," he said. "Then again, I've never been that bright."

"Don't say that!"

"Then you explain it to me. Is it that you're too insecure to explore a relationship with me, a *real* relationship, without you hiding behind C.J.? Or am I just an idiot for imagining something between us that was never really there?"

She bit her lip, tasted salt and realized she was crying. "So my choices are that I'm a chicken or that you're an idiot? Isn't there a none of the above?"

"There's *C*. People make mistakes."

She nodded vehemently, walking toward him. "I like *C*. I choose *C*. Dylan, I am truly sorry."

He took a step forward, intercepting her and pulling her into his embrace. "Don't ever lie to me again?"

"Lord, no. I'm terrible at it. I felt nauseous half the time. The other half," she admitted shyly, "I was just giddy to be with you."

That earned her a slow, thorough kiss. "Promise me one other thing?" he asked when he lifted his head.

Anything. She waited expectantly.

"If I get the coaching job and move to Mistletoe, don't help me decorate. I beg you."

She winced, remembering the gaudy accents she'd inflicted on his apartment.

"Where did you even find that butt-ugly throw rug? You didn't have enough time to get it special ordered from Vegas."

"The cupids?" In spite of herself, she grinned. "They were in this mega-discount bin of things that didn't sell on Valentine's Day."

"I can see why."

"I was so incensed when I heard that phone message, but it also seemed fitting," she admitted. "Deep down, part of me had wondered why a guy like you would be with me, and I suddenly realized that maybe it was all to teach me a lesson. That you were just—"

"Hey." He tipped her chin up with his index finger. "You're a beautiful, successful woman. Don't you think it's time to put Klutzy Chloe to bed?"

She looked into the eyes of the man she loved, the man who had helped her see herself as beautiful and successful, then startled him by tugging his hand. "Yes, please."

He chuckled, but there was more desire than amusement in his voice. "Lead the way."

As Coach Burton had predicted, once Dylan stated his clear interest in coming to work for Mistletoe High, the school board members were quick to pass a vote through, approving him for conditional employment with stipulations that he'd get further certification and education within the next year. Dylan had turned in his resignation notice at Channel Six and had sold his condo in Atlanta almost immediately—the building had a waiting list of interested tenants.

Tonight, Dylan was celebrating his impending return to Mistletoe with the people who meant the most to him.

"I still dread going back to school," Dylan complained to Chloe as they sat at the largest table in the Dixieland Diner.

"I promise to help you with your homework." She lowered her voice to a wickedly sexy register. "The trick is finding the right incentive program for each student."

"And you have some ideas about what might motivate me?" he teased.

"A few." She glanced over his shoulder, and he knew he'd have to wait until later to hear more. They had invited his mom, her parents, Nick, Shane, Natalie and Coach B. to join them for dinner. It looked as if Natalie and his mother had arrived simultaneously.

Dylan was surprised to see Chloe's expression turn wistful. "Everything okay?"

"Better than okay," she assured him. "It's just…I was thinking about someone I wish could have been here tonight."

He'd seen that nostalgic expression before. "Aunt Jane?"

"Yeah. Sometimes I feel like she was my fairy godmother. If she hadn't sent me that red dress, would I even have gone to the reunion? She would have loved you."

He squeezed her shoulder. "I love *you*. Chloe."

That brought a smile to her face. "I never get tired of hearing you say my name," she admitted.

Whatever response he would have made tapered off as they greeted Nat and Barb and then Shane and the coach. But even as Dylan talked to his friends, Chloe's words stayed at the back of his mind. Fairy godmother? A few months ago, he would have scoffed at that kind of fanciful notion. He'd been embittered by his shoulder injury and the loss of a career he loved and by the loss of his father. Even though they hadn't been close, Michael's death had cemented the fact that they'd never have a chance to repair their relationship. But now Dylan was too content to be bitter.

Natalie helped him find a small duplex to rent. Lilah and Tanner Waide had been living there while they waited for their house to be built and were now moving out. And for all his previous doubts about whether he'd make a good coach, Dylan was anxious to get started, to have the chance to live up to Coach Burton's example and Chloe's faith in him. The only time he'd ever felt life was a fairy tale was when he got called up to the majors, and that had been a short-lived euphoria. This, though—this felt solid and permanent.

He looked around the table at the faces of people he'd known all his life, people he loved. He knew they'd gorge themselves on chicken-fried steak and, later, key lime pie. They'd talk about ball and local events and laugh together, then he'd take Chloe home and make love to her until they fell asleep holding each other.

Dylan had never shared Chloe's enthusiasm for

books and had preferred sports biographies to fairy tales, but maybe she was onto something. He had to admit, this felt a hell of a lot like happily ever after.

* * * * *

Summer's coming to Mistletoe, GA, and things heat up between single dad Dr. Adam Varner and pet-sitter Brenna Pierce. Watch for MISTLETOE MOMMY by Tanya Michaels, coming August 2009, only from Harlequin American Romance!

*Celebrate 60 years of pure reading
pleasure with Harlequin®!*

*Step back in time and enjoy a sneak preview
of an exciting anthology from
Harlequin® Historical with*
THE DIAMONDS OF WELBOURNE MANOR

This compelling anthology features three stories
about the outrageous Fitzmanning sisters. Meet
Annalise, who is never at a loss for words… But
that can change with an unexpected encounter in
the forest.

*Available May 2009
from Harlequin® Historical.*

"I'm the illegitimate daughter of notoriously scandalous parents, Mr. Milford. Candidates for my hand are unlikely to be lining up at the gates."

"Don't be so quick to discount your charms, my dear. Or the charm of your substantial dowry. Or even your brothers' influence. There are as many reasons to marry as there are marriages."

Annalise snorted. "Oh, yes. Perhaps I shall marry for dynastic reasons, or perhaps for property or influence. After all, a loveless, practical marriage worked out so well for my mother."

"Well, you've routed me on that one. I can think of no suitable rejoinder." Ned rose to his feet and extended his hand. "And since that is the case, let me be the first to wish you a long and happy spinsterhood."

Her mouth gaped open. And then she laughed.

And he froze.

This was the first time, Ned realized. The first time he'd seen her eyes light up and her mouth curl. The first time he'd witnessed her features melded together in glorious accord to produce exquisite beauty.

Unbelievable what a change came over her face.
Unheard of what effect her throaty, rasping laughter
had on his body. It pounded a beat upon his ear, quickly
taken up by his pulse. It echoed through him, finally
residing in his stirring nether regions.

So easily she did it, awakened these sensations
within him—without any apparent effort at all. And she
had called him potentially dangerous? Clearly the intelligent thing for him to do would be to steer clear, to
leave her to the tender ministrations of Lord Peter
Blackthorne.

"You were right." She smiled up at him as she took
his hand and climbed to her feet. "I do feel better."

Ah, well. When had he ever chosen the intelligent path?

He did not relinquish her hand. He used it to pull her
in, close enough that he could feel the warmth of her.
"At the risk of repeating Lord Peter's mistake and an-
ticipating too much—may I ask if you'll be my partner
in battledore tomorrow?"

Her smiled dimmed. Her breath came a little faster. His
own had gone shallow, as if he'd just run a race—and lost.
He ran his gaze over the appealing lift of her brow and
the curious angle of her chin. His index finger twitched.

"I should like that," she said.

His finger trembled again and he lifted it, traced the
pink and tender shell of her ear, the unique sweep of her
jaw. Her pulse leaped beneath her skin, triggering his
own. Slowly he tilted her chin up, waiting for her to
object, to step back, to slap his hand away.

She did none of those eminently sensible things.
Which left him free to do the entirely impractical thing.

Baby soft, the skin of her lips. Her whole body trembled when he touched her there.

He leaned in. Her eyes closed, even as she stood straight against him, strung as tight as a bow. He pressed his mouth to hers. It was a soft kiss, sweet and chaste. And yet he was hot and hard and as ready as he'd ever been in his life.

She drew back a little. Sighed. Their breath mingled a moment before she slowly backed away.

"Oh," she breathed. Her dark eyes were full of wonder and something that looked like fear. He took a step toward her, but she only shook her head. His outstretched hand fell to his side as she turned to disappear into the wood. This was the first time, Ned realized. The first time, since he'd come to the house party at Welbourne Manor, that he'd seen her eyes light up.

* * * * *

Follow Ned and Annalise's story in May 2009 in
THE DIAMONDS OF WELBOURNE MANOR
Available May 2009 from Harlequin® Historical.

Available in the series romance section,
or in the historical romance section,
wherever books are sold.

**We'll be spotlighting a different series
every month throughout 2009
to celebrate our 60th anniversary.**

Look for Harlequin® Historical in May!

Celebrations begin with
a sumptuous Regency house party!

Join three scandalous sisters in

THE DIAMONDS OF
WELBOURNE MANOR

Glittering, scintillating, sensual fun
by Diane Gaston, Deb Marlowe
and Amanda McCabe.

**60 years of Harlequin,
600 years of romance
in Harlequin Historical!**

You're invited to join our Tell Harlequin Reader Panel!

By joining our new reader panel you will:

- Receive Harlequin® books—they are FREE and yours to keep with no obligation to purchase anything!
- Participate in fun online surveys
- Exchange opinions and ideas with women just like you
- Have a say in our new book ideas and help us publish the best in women's fiction

In addition, you will have a chance to win great prizes and receive special gifts!
See Web site for details. Some conditions apply.
Space is limited.

To join, visit us at
www.TellHarlequin.com.

THBPA0108

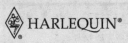

HARLEQUIN®

American ★ Romance®

LAURA MARIE ALTOM
The Marine's Babies

Men Made in America

Captain Jace Monroe is everything a Marine
should be—strong, brave and honorable. He's also
an instant father of twin baby girls he never knew
existed! Life gets even more complicated when he
finds himself attracted to Emma Stewart, his new
nanny. But can this sexy, fun-loving bachelor do
the right thing and become a family man?
Emma and the babies are counting on it!

Available in May
wherever books are sold.

LOVE, HOME & HAPPINESS

REQUEST YOUR FREE BOOKS!

2 FREE NOVELS PLUS 2
FREE GIFTS!

Love, Home & Happiness!

YES! Please send me 2 FREE Harlequin® American Romance® novels and my 2 FREE gifts (gifts are worth about $10). After receiving them, if I don't wish to receive any more books, I can return the shipping statement marked "cancel." If I don't cancel, I will receive 4 brand-new novels every month and be billed just $4.24 per book in the U.S. or $4.99 per book in Canada.* That's a savings of close to 15% off the cover price! It's quite a bargain! Shipping and handling is just 25¢ per book. I understand that accepting the 2 free books and gifts places me under no obligation to buy anything. I can always return a shipment and cancel at any time. Even if I never buy another book from Harlequin, the two free books and gifts are mine to keep forever.

154 HDN EEZK   354 HDN EEZV

Name	(PLEASE PRINT)
Address	Apt. #
City	State/Prov.	Zip/Postal Code

Signature (if under 18, a parent or guardian must sign)

Mail to the **Harlequin Reader Service:**
IN U.S.A.: P.O. Box 1867, Buffalo, NY 14240-1867
IN CANADA: P.O. Box 609, Fort Erie, Ontario L2A 5X3

Not valid to current subscribers of Harlequin® American Romance® books.

Want to try two free books from another line?
Call 1-800-873-8635 or visit www.morefreebooks.com.

* Terms and prices subject to change without notice. Prices do not include applicable taxes. N.Y. residents add applicable sales tax. Canadian residents will be charged applicable provincial taxes and GST. Offer not valid in Quebec. This offer is limited to one order per household. All orders subject to approval. Credit or debit balances in a customer's account(s) may be offset by any other outstanding balance owed by or to the customer. Please allow 4 to 6 weeks for delivery. Offer available while quantities last.

Your Privacy: Harlequin is committed to protecting your privacy. Our Privacy Policy is available online at www.eHarlequin.com or upon request from the Reader Service. From time to time we make our lists of customers available to reputable third parties who may have a product or service of interest to you. If you would prefer we not share your name and address, please check here. ☐

HAR09

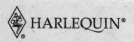

HARLEQUIN®

American ★ Romance®

COMING NEXT MONTH
Available May 12, 2009

#1257 THE MARINE'S BABIES by Laura Marie Altom
Men Made in America
Captain Jace Monroe is everything a marine should be—strong, brave and honorable. He's also an instant father of twin baby girls he didn't know existed! Life gets even more complicated when he finds himself attracted to Emma Stewart, his new nanny. But can this sexy, fun-loving bachelor do the right thing and become a family man? Emma and the baby brigade are counting on it!

#1258 ONCE A HERO by Lisa Childs
Citizen's Police Academy
Taking a bullet meant for someone else made Kent Terlecki a hero in the eyes of his fellow detectives. But Erin Powell doesn't see the brave cop behind the badge—just a man who put her brother in jail. Then the justice-seeking reporter enrolls in the Lakewood Citizen's Police Academy, looking for some answers…and finding the truth about an incredible man.

#1259 THE MAN MOST LIKELY by Cindi Myers
Bryan Perry is gorgeous and charismatic—the type of guy that Angela Krisova avoids. The full-figured gal has been jilted before. With her own successful business and fun social life, who needs to stir up trouble? So it's confusing when suddenly Bryan seems bent on pursuing *her*. Could this most unlikely of men be the one to win her heart?

#1260 HER VERY OWN FAMILY by Trish Milburn
Audrey York is running from a scandalous past and is determined to find peace in Willow Glen, Tennessee. Instead she finds Brady Witt, who is suspicious of her sudden interest in his widowed father. Audrey doesn't want her past to jeopardize Brady's and his dad's reputations, but she can't help hoping for what she's always wanted—a family of her own.

www.eHarlequin.com

HARCNMBPA0409